GHETTO TEARS

Story by
Tamara Prince-Greer
Screenplay by Marlon Jones

ISBN 979-8-35094-667-3

DARKNESS. The faint sound of SNIFFLING and CRYING can be heard.

FADE IN:

EXT. APARTMENT COMPLEX COURTYARD — NIGHT

A modestly built female figure slowly drags herself through the red brick courtyard. Is she homeless... drunk? She is definitely UNSTEADY as she looks down at her cellphone.

With a gut-wrenching SOB she drops her phone in a bush and rushes toward one of the apartment doors.

INT. APARTMENT — MOMENTS LATER

The WEEPING female enters this cold, dark dungeon... on a mission to find something... hopefully, not people because she is clearly ALL ALONE in this sterile and uninviting space.

INT. BEDROOM 1 - CONTINUOUS

She goes into a bedroom, which is obviously that of a TEENAGE GIRL, grabs a scratch pad and scribbles a note on it. As she scans the room, she notices a SHELF OF TROPHIES but CRIES as she realizes that several are missing. She quickly rushes out of the room.

INT. BEDROOM 2 - MOMENTS LATER

Breathing heavily, the girl enters the room, heads toward the closet but stops in her tracks as she stares at a PHOTO of a MAN and WOMAN smiling happily... hanging on the wall.

She grabs the photo off the wall... looks at it for a moment. Then suddenly, she angrily smashes it on the floor and goes into the closet.

INT. CLOSET - CONTINUOUS

Seen from behind, the girl frantically searches the closet... opening and tossing shoe boxes off the top shelf until... she reaches into one shoe box and stops... pulling out a **GLOCK 9MM.**

As she turns around... this is the first time her face is revealed... MIA REYNOLDS, 16, plain-Jane in the way she's dressed but her physical beauty is obvious even through the streaming tears and messed up make-up.

As Mia studies the gun, her expression fluctuates between fear and peace.

Mia begins to breathe hard again, disengages the SAFETY, and then turns off the light. In complete darkness, Mia mumbles to herself and her breathing becomes frenetic... almost like she's hyperventilating and sobbing at the same time.

Suddenly... BANG!!! The room briefly lights up from the gun blast!!!

Immediately, events from Mia's life play out in **flashbacks.**

MONTAGE:

INT. RUN DOWN APARTMENT - DAY

Young Mia (5 or 6) in an empty, run down apartment watching people doing drugs.

INT. SMALL HOUSE - DAY

Young Mia (7 or 8) in a house full of people
interacting with each other... she is watching
sadly as young girls her age play together but
look in her direction and smirk at her.

EXT. APARTMENT COMPLEX COURTYARD - EVENING

Young Mia (8 or 9) being physically disciplined
by a man while a woman looks on.

INT. LUNCH ROOM - DAY

Young Mia (10 or 11) is a loner at school... eat-
ing at a table all by herself.

INT. SCHOOL AUDITORIUM - NIGHT

Older Mia (12 or 13) on stage receiving a trophy
and looking into the audience but not seeing anyone there to support her.

INT. LOCAL DINER - NIGHT

High school aged Mia (15) sitting at a table with
a woman and a man in a low budget diner... the
man smiling at the woman while caressing Mia's
leg under the table.

INT. SCHOOL HALLWAY - DAY

High school aged Mia (15) walking down the hallway and getting taunted and teased by a group of
girls... she is visibly upset as tears stream
down her face.

INT. MIA'S ROOM - NIGHT

High school aged Mia (16) in her bed... visibly
sad and withdrawn as a man zips up his pants,
grabs his blue uniform jacket, and walks out of
her room.

INT. APARTMENT - NIGHT

Mia (16), in the same apartment where she shot
herself, is being yelled at by a man while a
woman looks on... then she gets kicked out of the
apartment... with the woman staying silent.

EXT. NEIGHBORHOOD STREET - LATE NIGHT

Mia (16)... wandering the streets... alone...
crying...

INT. CLOSET - NIGHT BANG!!!

END FLASHBACK MONTAGE

EXT. CLOSET - NIGHT

A shrill scream of terror fills the apartment as
LINDA DANIELS, 30's, finds Mia's lifeless and
bloody body laying on the floor.

Instead of going to Mia, Linda rushes out of the room and out of the apartment into the court-yard screaming!

EXT. APARTMENT COMPLEX COURTYARD — MOMENTS LATER

                    LINDA
  Help me! Oh my God! Somebody... Help!

Suddenly, several lights from different apartments turn on and people hurry out their doors to see Linda... a well put together woman with expe-rience, hard experience, in her piercing brown eyes. She's visibly shaking but is it because of what she saw or... something else?

                    LINDA (CONT'D)
    It's... Mia.

The courtyard is now full of people... men, women, and children alike... the perfect picture of a tight-knit community.

TINA PARKER, 40's, not beautiful but not hideous either, rushes over to Linda with obvious moth-erly concern.

                    TINA
  What about Mia, Linda?

                    LINDA
  (Struggling) She's... dead.

KEVIN PARKER, late 40's, a rugged, blue collar man's man with secrets in his eyes, overhears the conversation and turns to the crowd.

                        KEVIN
    Somebody call 911!

Kevin immediately rushes to Linda's apartment. Tina ushers a reluctant Linda toward
the apartment.

INT. CLOSET — MOMENTS LATER

Kevin kneels next to Mia's still body, holding
her wrist.

                    KEVIN (CONT'D)
    She's not dead. I can feel her pulse.

Tina gently nudges Linda toward the closet but
Linda resists.

                        LINDA
    (Sobbing)
    I can't... I... just... can't.

                        TINA
    Your baby girl needs you right now.

Linda unwillingly goes to Mia as Kevin moves out
of her way. Linda takes Mia's hand and immediately has a FLASHBACK to a time not too long ago.

INT. APARTMENT — NIGHT

The end of the encounter where Mia is being
yelled at and kicked out of the apartment by a
man is replaying. Except this time, we recognize
LINDA as the woman who remained silent.

As Mia exits the apartment, Linda looks on sadly and sheds a tear.

END FLASHBACK

INT. CLOSET — CONTINUOUS

Back in real time, Linda's face is streaming with tears as she looks down at her daughter's motion-less body.

EXT. APARTMENT COMPLEX COURTYARD — MOMENTS LATER

Blaring sirens overpower the loud chatter of the concerned neighbors as emergency vehicles arrive in the courtyard.

A POLICE OFFICER races to the center of the crowd.

> POLICE OFFICER
> Heard on the scanner that a woman has been shot. Where is she?

BROOKE HILL, 50's, a beautiful, kind soul, steps forward.

> BROOKE
> She's just a girl, Officer... a young girl. Her apartment is this way.

Brooke leads the Officer toward the Daniels' apartment.

EXT. CLOSET — MOMENTS LATER

The Officer enters the room and sees Linda holding Mia's hand. As he scans the scene he sees the gun next to Mia. He approaches Linda.

> POLICE OFFICER
> Ma'am, I'm Officer King and I'm sorry but I have to ask you a few questions.

Linda doesn't respond audibly... she just nods.

> POLICE OFFICER (CONT'D)
> What is your relationship to the victim?

> LINDA
> My daughter.

> POLICE OFFICER
> Is that your gun?

Linda looks at the gun and shakes her head.

> LINDA
> My husband's.

> POLICE OFFICER
> Did you discover the victim?

Linda nods.

> POLICE OFFICER (CONT'D)
> Was there any sign of forced entry into the apartment when you arrived?

Linda shakes her head.

POLICE OFFICER (CONT'D)
This appears to be self-inflicted. Do you know of any reason why your daughter would do this?

Linda's demeanor immediately changes. She becomes tense and begins to weep and shake her head as the EMT's enter the room.

INT. VAN — NIGHT

SHANNON PRICE, 30's, a sophisticated but no non-sense kinda gal listens to the police scanner from the passenger seat. She tries to hide her physical beauty behind non-prescription glasses but that's like trying to dim the brightness of her soul.

SHANNON
(To the driver)

Did you hear that? Something's happening in your neighborhood.

The driver, DAVID RICHARDS, 40's, large and burly like a bear... and hairy like one too... shoots back a very telling response.

DAVID
Something's always happening in my neighborhood.

EXT. APARTMENT COMPLEX COURTYARD — MOMENTS LATER

The crowd in the courtyard has grown as more people from the neighborhood have arrived to see what's going on.

Indistinct chatter... neighbor talking to neighbor wearing real looks of concern. Feels like a loving, tight-knit community.

The crowd parts as a CHANNEL 9 NEWS VAN drives into the courtyard.

David and Shannon exit the van and spring right into action. Shannon, microphone in hand, approaches the crowd as David follows behind her with his TV camera.

MIKE MURPHY, still dressed in his MAILMAN uniform sees David and crosses to him... or better yet, waddles to him as his short, stubby legs can only carry his equally stocky body so fast. Luckily for Mike mail is no longer delivered on foot.

                    MIKE
    If you're looking for news to report... the
    Reynolds kid shot herself.

Shannon jumps in... Shoves the microphone into Mike's face.

                    SHANNON
    Excuse me, Sir. Did you say, "Kid"?

                    MIKE
    Yes, Ma'am. A high school girl.

                    SHANNON
    Do we know why she may have done this?

Mike scans the crowd, shakes his head in sadness.

                    MIKE
She always seemed so... happy. Our
community is close. Can't believe nobody
saw this coming.

                  SHANNON
And what is your name, Sir.

                    MIKE
No comment.

Shannon and David peer at Mike curiously, then at
each other as Mike sadly slides away.

Shannon moves into position in front of David and
gives him the signal to begin rolling the filming.

                  SHANNON
This is Shannon Price, News 9, reporting
from the 103rd block of Vermont where a
shooting involving a teen aged girl has
been reported.

Another neighbor, CONSTANCE HARPER, probably 50's
but trying her best to prove 50 is the new 30,
approaches Shannon.

              SHANNON (CONT'D)
Ma'am, can you tell us what happened?

                 CONSTANCE
Don't call me Ma'am. I'm Connie. And what
happened is a tragedy. I don't understand
why she would do this.

                  SHANNON
What about her parents? Do they have a good
relationship? Does she have a boyfriend?

CONSTANCE
Her parents are great people but they didn't
let Mia date.

SHANNON
Any particular reason why?

CONSTANCE
Even though Mia looks like a woman physically,
mentally... she's just a kid.

SHANNON
Where are her parents now?

CONSTANCE
Her mother found the body and John isn't
here yet.

Suddenly, a man frantically bursts onto the
scene...

JOHN
Where is she, Connie? Is she dead?

Shannon looks on as JOHN DANIELS, late 30's,
agonizes over an answer he doesn't want. Even in
panic mode John's charisma and charm are undeni-
able. He's a man that most likely gets what he
wants because of his physical attractiveness or
his silver tongue or... both.

CONSTANCE
She's still in your apartment.

Immediately, John rushes off as Connie's
gaze lingers.

CONSTANCE (CONT'D)
(To Shannon)
That's Mia's step-dad, John, and... My man crush.

Shannon stares at Constance who wears a girl-ish grin.

EXT. APARTMENT — MOMENTS LATER

Emergency personnel are coming out the Daniels' apartment carefully pushing the gurney. John sees and frantically races to it but... stops in his track when he spots Linda being led out of the apartment by Tina Parker.

John bypasses the gurney and darts to Linda!

JOHN
Oh my God, Baby! I thought it was you! I thought it was you.

John plants several kisses on Linda's face. It's obvious this is the best sight he could have hoped for.

Linda doesn't react or respond to the barrage of kisses... she is numb... shock is setting in.

JOHN (CONT'D)
You okay?

LINDA
(Voice shaking) No... Mia...

Finally, John inches toward the gurney and sees Mia but shows no emotion.

EXT. APARTMENT COMPLEX COURTYARD — CONTINUOUS

The EMT's approach the ambulance with the gurney and load it into the back. They beckon for Linda to get into the back of the ambulance with them but she remains frozen in place.

> EMT 1
>
> Come on, Mrs. Daniel. Your daughter needs you right now.

> EMT 2
>
> These could be your last moments with her.

> LINDA
>
> (Sobbing) I... can't.

Shannon looks on curiously... trying to make sense of what's going on with Linda.

John grabs Linda's hand, looks her in the eyes, and kisses her.

> JOHN
>
> You can do this, Babe. You can. I need you to do this. For me... Mia.
>
> John gives a knowing look to Linda who snaps out of her state of shock and climbs into the back of the ambulance.

> JOHN (CONT'D)
>
> That's my girl. I'll meet you at the hospital. Don't worry... I'll take care of everything like I usually do.

Linda flashes a halfhearted smile as the EMTs close the ambulance door.

As the ambulance pulls off slowly and passes through the crowd of concerned neighbors and community Looky-Lous, the EMTs continue to work on Mia.

Mia is unconscious but it's like she can see what's going on as she gives her rundown...

> MIA (V.O.)
> All these people... full of concern. Or... are they just hoping that their secrets die with me?
> (Smirks)
> And these strangers... doing their best to keep me alive.
> (Scoffs)
> Please... just leave me alone. (Beat)
> Because if you knew what I have lived through... you would be kind enough to just... let... me... die.

CUT TO BLACK:

INT. HOSPITAL WAITING ROOM — NIGHT

Waiting rooms are depressing by nature but this one... makes a funeral service look lively.

Tears, fears, and shock are plastered on the faces of all who sit, stand, or pace anxiously.

PEYTON "PK" KRAMER, 16, is the only non-minority in the place but her blonde hair and green eyes don't make her stand out more than the fact that

she is on her knees, praying, in a corner... face
wet with tears.

                    PK
    Lord, please spare Mia. She doesn't deserve
    to go to hell. You know her heart. She
    just has some demons she's dealing with but
    she's a good person.

BEGIN FLASHBACK

EXT. HIGH SCHOOL — DAY

A slightly younger PK, wearing a skirt longer
than girls her age would normally wear, hurries
away from the school building as she is being
pursued/harassed by a black guy who is twice her
size. She is visibly upset as the guy peppers her
with sexually explicit statements.

PK is on the verge of tears when Mia, wearing
baggy sweat pants and an equally baggy blouse
that doesn't match, gets between the guy and PK.

                    MIA
    Leave her alone, LeMarcus. She don't want
    nothing you got.

PK hears this confrontation but continues to
rush away.

                  LEMARCUS
    What about you, Mia? (Getting closer)

    I heard you want what everybody got. How
    about another baby?

Immediately, Mia becomes FURIOUS.

> MIA
>
> You don't know what the fuck you're talking about. Asshole!

Mia violently shoves LeMarcus but he doesn't budge as he is just so much bigger than she is. He laughs at Mia and she sprints away... completely hurt and humiliated.

PK sees Mia and runs toward her.

> PK
>
> Excuse me! Excuse me!

Mia hears PK calling but doesn't stop running until she has to... at a stop light. This allows PK to catch up with Mia.

> PK (CONT'D)
>
> (Out of breath) Thank you.
>
> (Breathes deeply)
>
> Thank you for that back there.

Mia doesn't respond.

> PK (CONT'D)
>
> I'm Peyton but my friends call me PK.

Mia doesn't look like she needs or wants any friends right now as she is visibly shaking.

> PK (CONT'D)
>
> I don't know what he said to you but that guy's obviously an idiot.

Mia stops shaking and finally responds... angrily.

                         MIA
     He don't know me!

                         PK
     (Warmly smiling)
     Is it okay if I get to know you? Me and
     my family just moved here and I don't know
     anyone. And... Anyone who would stand up to
     Andre the Giant for me... I want on my side.

Mia peers at PK curiously.

                         MIA
     What you know about Andre the Giant?

Mia sheds a slight smile and PK flashes a grin
back at her fellow wrestling fan.

END FLASHBACK

INT. HOSPITAL WAITING ROOM — CONTINUOUS

                         PK
     In Jesus' name, I pray... Amen.

PK is no longer crying but instead, she's wearing
a nostalgic smile.

Tina Parker is sitting in a chair as her two
younger daughters are draped on her... asleep.
Tina wears the look of motherly concern all over
her face.

As she rubs the heads of her two children she
goes back to a time when Mia interacted with her
kids in the courtyard.

EXT. APARTMENT COMPLEX COURTYARD — DAY

Mia stands against a tree hiding her eyes and counting as Tina Parker's kids scramble to find hiding places.

                    MIA
     3... 2... 1... ready or not... here I come.

Mia spots the poorly hidden kids immediately but... pretends like she can't find them and wanders around the courtyard.

                MIA (CONT'D)
     Are you behind this trash can?

Mia hears the children giggle as she lunges to look behind a trash can.

                MIA (CONT'D)
     You must be under this car!

Mia bends down to look under one of the cars in one of the carports as the kids laugh again.

                MIA (CONT'D)
     Okay... the last place two good hiders could
     be is... in your room.

As Mia walks toward the Parker's apartment, the kid's race toward a makeshift fortress made of cardboard boxes and old blankets and sheets.

Mia makes eye contact with Tina who watches from the window.

                        MIA (CONT'D)
I don't know, Mrs. Parker... they really
disappeared this time. I can't find them.

Tina smiles and Mia smiles back.

                        TINA
I guess they don't want these treats.
(Beat)
Here. You take 'em, Mia.

Tina hands Mia two deliciously gooey RICE
CRISPY TREATS.

                        MIA
Thanks, Mrs. Parker. I'm going to eat these
in the Fortress.

Mia smiles as she sashays toward the makeshift
fortress. As soon as she enters the fortress, the
two kids jump up and yell tauntingly...

                        KIDS
You couldn't find us!

Mia laughs and gives the kids the treats.

                        MIA
I don't know why I didn't look here first.
This is your favorite hiding place.

Tina smiles as she witnesses the positive scene
but... Tina isn't the only one observing... Kevin
Parker looks on smiling too... intently.

After a few moments, Kevin approaches Mia and the kids.

                    KEVIN
Thank you for being so good with our kids.
They really like you.

Mia flashes an uncomfortable grin at Kevin which triggers another FLASHBACK for Tina.

INT. THE PARKER APARTMENT — NIGHT

Mia sits nervously on the couch in the living room as Tina enters from the hallway.

                    TINA
Now that the kids are asleep... I can actually listen to you. What's wrong, Mia? What's on your mind?

You can tell me, Sweetheart.

Mia looks like she wants to say something but... she just breaks down... sobbing.

Tina gets up to console Mia... rubbing her back.

                    TINA (CONT'D)
Whatever it is... it's going to be okay. I promise.

                    MIA
I need your help, Mrs. Parker.

                    TINA
Whatever you need, Sweetheart.

Kevin opens the front door, walks in and stares peculiarly at the odd scene.

                    KEVIN
     Is everything okay?

Mia hops up suddenly, puts on a brave face,
and...

                    MIA
     Thank you, Mrs. Parker. I gotta go.

                    TINA
     It's okay, Mia... you can stay if you
     need to.

Mia doesn't respond as she rushes out the
front door.

END FLASHBACK

INT. HOSPITAL WAITING ROOM — CONTINUOUS

Tears are now streaming down Tina's face. Brooke
Hill crosses to Tina and gives her some tissue to
wipe her eyes. It is obvious that Brooke has been
crying too as her BIG BROWN EYES are puffy.

Brooke looks down at Tina's kids and one of them
pulls their jacket over their head to hide their
face... triggering a memory.

EXT. THE HILL APARTMENT — DAY

A young 40's BROOKE HILL sits on her back porch
smoking a cigarette and listening to her portable
CD player.

As the song she was listening to ends, she thinks
she hears something but the next song starts and
she relaxes again....and turns up the music.

After a few moments, Brooke stands up and attentively scans her surroundings. She1 definitely
hears something.

Brooke slowly walks down the stairs of her porch
and toward the back of the property... in the
direction of a small rickety tool shed.

As Brooke approaches the shed, she hears whimpering. She opens the shed but doesn't see anyone
and the whimpering stops immediately.

Brooke takes a closer look... moving a peculiarly
placed wheelbarrow and revealing... young (5 or
6) Mia hiding her face under her jacket.

Brooke picks up the frightened girl and hugs her
tightly... young Mia just soaking up this strang-
er's affection.

END FLASHBACK

INT. HOSPITAL WAITING ROOM — CONTINUOUS

Brooke wears a smirk as her focus is on MISS
CLARITA JONES, 60's. She might have white hair,
wear pantyhose, and walk with a cane but she
ain't nobody's Grandma... call her that and you
just might get popped.

Miss Clarita spots a Nurse leaving the waiting room after talking to another family. As the
Nurse walks past Miss Clarita, she holds out her
cane... almost tripping the nurse.

                    MISS CLARITA
        (Creole accent)

        Aw, Bay-bee, you were walking too fast.
        Didn't mean to do that.

The Nurse doesn't buy it but
remains professional.

                MISS CLARITA (CONT'D)
        My daughter is the mama of the victim. When
        can I see her?

                    NURSE
        You mean, your grand-daughter, Ma'am?

                    MISS CLARITA
        well.... family is complicated.

The Nurse doesn't know where to file that comment
as she frowns at the unemotional matriarch.

                    NURSE
        Only immediately family can see her tonight
        but regular visiting hours are from 8am
        to 9pm.

                (Probing)
        I can take you in now, if you'd like since
        you're her grandmother.

                    MISS CLARITA
                (Avoiding)
        Nah, its okay. This her Mama's time to spend
        with her. Besides... my heart can only take
        so much in one day.

                    NURSE
        Your heart? I can believe it.

The Nurse walks away in disbelief. Miss Clarita struggles out of her chair and approaches three girls sitting across the room looking at their phones... all watching the same video... Mia hurrying down a school hallway as uproarious laughter is rained down on her.

                    MISS CLARITA
     Let's go girls.

STEPHANIE, 17, TASHA, 16, and TRACY, 15...
The COLLINS

Sisters look up at Miss Clarita simultaneously. These girls' physical appearance resembles that of a world-touring singing group with millions of fans but emotionally... they are broken down.

Stephanie quickly exits the video and stands up.

                    TRACY
     I want to see Mia. Tell her I'm -

                    STEPHANIE
          (Cutting her off)
     You heard the nurse... regular visiting hours are tomorrow.

Tracy looks at Tasha who quickly studies Stephanie's scowl.

                    TASHA
     Tomorrow, Trace.

Tasha and Tracy get up and all three girls follow Miss Clarita out of the waiting room.

INT. HOSPITAL HALLWAY — MOMENTS LATER

John and Linda stand in the hallway with DOCTOR
GREEN. John is intense and Linda looks... lost.
John listens closely as the Doctor speaks.

> DOCTOR GREEN
>
> Mia suffered a penetrating wound and we need
> to perform surgery right away so she can
> have a chance to live.

> JOHN
>
> A penetrating wound?

> DOCTOR GREEN
>
> That's where the bullet breaches the
> cranium but doesn't exit. We need to get
> the bullet out.

> JOHN
>
> What are her chances of survival?

> DOCTOR GREEN
>
> Gunshot wound head trauma is fatal about
> 90% of the time with most victims dying
> prior to getting to the hospital.
>
> (Beat)
>
> Your girl has already beat the odds and
> seems to be a fighter so we need to get her
> into surgery now so she can keep fighting.

Linda remains silent but John is trying to
wrap his brain around all of this.

> JOHN
>
> If she survives... what will her life be
> like? Will she be normal?

The Doctor frowns...

                    DOCTOR GREEN
I don't think you understand the importance
of every minute right now, Mr. Daniels.

(Looks at Linda)

Your daughter most likely will suffer from
the effects of this for the rest of her life
but... she will be alive.

Linda begins to cry and John moves to hug her.
She poises herself and...

                       LINDA
Will she have her memory? (Breaks down)
She's got a great memory.

                       JOHN
What do you need from us, Doctor, to get Mia
into surgery?

                    DOCTOR GREEN
Parental consent papers signed since she's
a minor and it's always good to have some
extra blood on hand.

John looks at Linda who looks away somberly.

                       JOHN
(Uncomfortably)

I'm not the biological father and my wife
doesn't do well with needles at all.

                    DOCTOR GREEN
Well, we will only draw your blood, Mrs.
Daniels, if we absolutely need it.

(Smiles at Linda) Sound good?

Linda nods reluctantly.

INT. OPERATING ROOM — LATER

The surgical staff, led by Doctor Green, studies three screens that show different views or Mia's cranium.

>   MIA (V.O.)
> How ironic... why all the attention now? Trying to redeem yourselves, doctors? You should have done this the last time I was here.

Mia's body jerks... she's having a seizure. The doctors have to restrain her and strap her arms down... revealing the SCARS ON HER WRISTS.

>   MIA (V.O.)
> Now you want to try to save the poor girl who blew her brains out?
> (MORE)

>   MIA (V.O.) (CONT'D)
> (Scoffs)
> Do you all feel guilty? Are all the people in the waiting room here to see if I live... or if I die?
> (Laughs)
> I'm sure many of them are hoping that I succeed in what I did so that their secrets die with me.
> (Solemnly)
> But if I'm being honest... I wish I was stronger. Strong enough to deal with the

crap that was put on me at an early age...
and keep on movin.'

(Beat)

But that's hard to do when everybody around
you has no hope.

As the doctors are about to begin the surgery...
a BRIGHT LIGHT illuminates the entire operating room.

DISSOLVE TO:

REPLAY of earlier FLASHBACK with a reveal.

INT. RUN DOWN APARTMENT — DAY

Young Mia (5 or 6) is in an empty, rundown apartment watching people doing drugs. One of the
women staggers toward Mia... it is LINDA and she
looks like a classic "dope fiend."

                    LINDA
    You hungry, Baby? Mama's hungry. Let's go.
    I'ma make us some food.

Linda grabs Mia's hand and as she turns to walk
away... she stumbles and crashes to the ground.
The other druggies laugh but Mia attends to
her mother... making sure that she's breathing and not seriously hurt... like she's done
this before.

                    MIA (V.O.)
    Taking care of the person who was supposed
    to take care of me made me grow up way
    too fast.

INT. APARTMENT — NIGHT

Young Mia (6 or 7) stands on a stool in front of the stove cooking... while Linda sits on the couch under a blanket... shivering... probably from withdrawals.

Mia grabs a bowl from the cabinet, grabs the pot she's cooking in, and struggles to pour some soup into the bowl as the pot is large compared to how petite Mia is.

Mia carries the hot soup to her mother using wet sponges as oven mitts. Linda sits up as Mia puts the bowl in front of her and... Opens her mouth! Mia grabs the spoon and feeds her!

                    LINDA
Mmmmmm... This is good, Me-me. (Smiles at Mia)

You are the best thing that has ever happened to me.

Mia smiles and soaks in this sentimental moment as she keeps feeding her mother.

                   MIA (V.O.)
I was exposed to things that most adults shouldn't experience.

EXT. NEIGHBORHOOD STREET — DAY

Young Mia (8 or 9) and Linda walk along the side-walk talking and having a good time despite the fact that they are not in a good part of town.

As they approach an alley, Linda's demeanor changes... she gets antsy.

MIA

You okay, Mama?

Linda bends down and looks Mia in the eyes.

LINDA

There's a man down this alley. I need you to go give him the watch I gave you last week and he's gonna give you something for me.

MIA

No, Mama, I like this watch.

LINDA

(Sternly)

I'll get you another one.

MIA

I don't want another one.

LINDA

(Angrily) What did I say?!

Mia starts to cry... infuriating Linda even more.

LINDA (CONT'D)

(Yelling)

What are you crying about? You didn't buy that watch! I did! And if I want to give it away... I will!

Mia is now SOBBING. Linda looks at her for a moment then... takes the watch off Mia's arm... causing Mia to cry hysterically.

                    LINDA (CONT'D)
Why can't you ever just do what I say?

(Scoffs)

You are the worst thing that has ever
happened to me.

Linda turns and walks down the alley... leaving
Mia devastated.

                    MIA (V.O.)
But what choice did I really have?

INT. APARTMENT — NIGHT

Young Mia (12 or 13) is in her room... singing.
Linda stands by the door smiling at her talented daughter.

                    LINDA
You sound so good, Me-Me. Just like Alicia
Keys. That's why you won that talent show.

(Somberly)

Sorry, I couldn't be there. I had my meeting.

Mia nods with understanding.

                    LINDA (CONT'D)
And tonight is a big one... Day 60. You have
to come with me.

Mia frowns.

                    MIA
Auditions for the school musical are tonight
and I really want to go because people are

saying that I shouldn't have won the talent show. Getting the lead role would shut them up.

Linda's smile immediately disappears.

> LINDA
>
> I know that's important to you, Me- Me, but this is huge for me. 60 days clean? I couldn't have done it without you. I need you there.

Mia remains silent. Linda sees this and lays on the guilt trip.

> LINDA (CONT'D)
>
> You don't want me to fall off again, do you?

Mia knows she can't say no so... she forces a smile.

> MIA
>
> Of course not, Mama. I'll go with you.

> LINDA
>
> (Smiling again)
>
> Thank you, Baby. You're the best thing that has ever happened to me.

> MIA (V.O.)
>
> Like I said... I didn't really have a choice.

END FLASHBACK

EXT. HOSPITAL PARKING LOT — DAY

The News Nine Van is parked in the lot with a small crowd huddled together in front of it.

Shannon is in front of the group as David points the camera at her.

                    SHANNON
     We're here at Huntington Memorial Hospital
     following up on the tragic story we broke
     last night about a young girl who allegedly
     tried to commit suicide... and the community
     who is in shock because of it.

     (Beat)

     We are not releasing the name of the victim
     as she is a minor and her parents have not
     given permission to do so.

Shannon walks to the crowd and sees an oddity...
PAUL KRAMER, 50's, P.K's father, dressed in a
black 3-Piece Suit. Paul is as slim as can be
considered healthy for a man but towers over most
people in the crowd.

Shannon approaches Paul who's per ma-smile may
be attributed to the BIBLE he holds tightly in
his hands.

                 SHANNON (CONT'D)
     (To Paul)

     Shannon Price News Nine. What brings you
     here, Sir?

                 PASTOR KRAMER
     I'm Pastor Paul Kramer of the Greater
     Bethany Baptist Church.

     (Beat)

     This tragedy happened in our community so
     I'm here to support.

(Beat)

And... My daughter is close to the young lady.

                    SHANNON
Reports have come in that the young woman
survived the lengthy surgery last night but
is unresponsive as of yet.

                  PASTOR KRAMER
It's a miracle she's even alive. (Raising
his Bible)

Let's just keep praying for her... as a
community. This is a wake up call.

                    SHANNON
A wake up call, indeed. (Beat)

I'm Shannon Price, News Nine, and we'll
continue to update this story as it unfolds.

Shannon pauses for a moment, then gives the "cut"
sign to David.

She marches over to David with a determined look
in her eyes.

                 SHANNON (CONT'D)
There's something more to this story,
David... I can feel it.

                    DAVID
Why do you think that?

                    SHANNON
Call it reporter's gut or... women's
intuition but... something doesn't add up
here. Nobody knows why this girl would try
to kill herself?

(Smirks)

Somebody knows something... and I'm going to find out what it is.

David shakes his head and scowls.

                    DAVID
     I've seen that look before. Not... good...
     just be careful... remember what happened
     the last time...

Shannon peers intensely at David and he stares back... with equal intensity.

INT. HOSPITAL — ICU — DAY

John and Linda sit in chairs restlessly study-ing Mia who is hooked up to several machines. The only movement from Mia is the machine that is moving her chest to make her breathe.

Suddenly, Linda thinks she sees something and snaps out of her daze.

                    LINDA
     Did you see that? She moved her arm.

John shakes his head in disbelief.

                    JOHN
     I didn't see any movement.

                    LINDA
     (Insisting) No... She moved it.

     (Beat)

     See! There it is again.

John realizes what's going on.

                    JOHN
You should get some rest, Babe. It's been a
long night. I think your eyes are playing
tricks on you.

(Smirks)

I know you feel bad but... we can't fill
ourselves with false hope.

(MORE)

               JOHN (CONT'D)
(Sadly)

Because... she might never wake up.

Linda drops her eyes and returns to her almost
catatonic state as Doctor Green enters.

               DOCTOR GREEN
Mr. and Mrs. Daniels... we were able to
remove the bullet from Mia's brain but...
it caused major damage. Damage we can't
quantify right now.

                    JOHN
What do you mean, "can't quantify"?

               DOCTOR GREEN
Mia's GCS score is 4 so we can't really measure
her brain stem neurological function.

                    JOHN
(Frustrated)

We don't know what any of that means, Doctor.

               DOCTOR GREEN
The Glasgow Coma Scale measures a patient's
level of consciousness. A score of seven or

less... the patient is considered to be in a coma.

                    JOHN
So Mia's in a coma?

Doctor Green nods.

                 DOCTOR GREEN
And until she comes out of it... we won't know the extent of the damage.

                    LINDA
Will she come out if it, Doctor?

                 DOCTOR GREEN
Even though Mia survived the surgery... due to the trajectory of the bullet and the damage it caused... her chances of ultimate survival are very low.

  (MORE)

              DOCTOR GREEN (CONT'D)
(beat)

The next 48 hours are critical.

so.... you might want to have people start to say their "goodbyes."

This visibly upsets Linda who breaks down and runs out of the room sobbing. John quickly follows to console her.

                   MIA (V.O.)
Alone again... I guess I should be used to it by now.

INT. APARTMENT — ROOM — NIGHT

Linda is uncharacteristically happy as she dances around her room in a ratty bathrobe. Young Mia (13 or 14) notices and immediately takes on a posture of concern... worried as to what has caused Linda to act this way.

                    MIA
    Are you okay, Mom?

                    LINDA
    I'm great, Me-Me! Why you asking?

                    MIA
    It's just... I mean... I've never seen you
    this happy...

                    LINDA
    (Cutting her off)
    Sober? Is that what you were going to say?
    (Smiles)
    Don't worry. I didn't fall of the wagon.

Mia doesn't believe Linda. She still looks at her skeptically. Linda sees this and crosses to Mia.

                LINDA (CONT'D)
    (Blowing in Mia's face) See! No drinks.
    (Opens her eyes wide)
    Look at my eyes. Normal pupils. (Smiles)
    I told you, Me-Me. I'm clean.

Mia is still suspicious but backs off a little.

                    MIA
    Then where did this Beyonce come from?

Linda laughs.

                    LINDA
    Bey has a date! That's right!

Linda stands in front of a mirror... putting
on makeup.

                    MIA
    And you're just telling me?

                    LINDA
    It just happened today. Out of nowhere.

                    MIA
    How? Who is he?

Linda finishes her makeup, takes off her robe, and
saunters to the closet like she's on a catwalk.

                    LINDA
    His name is John and I met him at the
    shelter today. He's the new director... and
    he is fine!

The doorbell rings. Linda and Mia hear it and
look at each other.

                    LINDA (CONT'D)
    And... A little early!

Linda rushes to finish getting ready.

                    LINDA (CONT'D)
Go get the door and tell him I'll be
right out.

                    MIA
(Hesitantly)
Okay... but what about dinner?

                    LINDA
Girl, you cook better than me. Make yourself
something. Mama gotta get her groove on.

Mia leaves the room to go answer the door.

INT. APARTMENT — LIVING ROOM — CONTINUOUS

Mia opens the door and a VERY DAPPER John stand
at the door holding a dozen RED ROSES.

                    JOHN
Well, hello there, Mia.

John flashes his characteristic charming smile.

                    JOHN (CONT'D)
Your Mother told me so much about you today.
You sound like an incredible young woman.

Mia kinda blushes at the compliment but turns
away so John doesn't see just as Linda enters...
wearing huge smile.

                    LINDA
John! So, you met my little girl, huh?

                    JOHN
I did... and she's prettier than
you described.

Linda turns to Mia and sheds a warm grin. Then she turns back to John.

                    LINDA
    Do you always know exactly what to say?

    John grins bashfully...

                    JOHN
    I just speak the truth. And the truth is...
    we better go before we're late.

Linda nods. Turns to Mia.

                    LINDA
    You know the drill... call Mrs. Parker if
    you need something. Make sure everything is
    locked. And don't stay up too late.

(Kisses Mia's forehead) Good night.

Linda turns to John and walks toward the door.

                    JOHN
    (To Mia)
    I'll take good care of her.

John flashes a slick smile and then he and Linda exit the apartment... leaving Mia all alone.

INT. HOSPITAL — ICU — DAY

John stands in the corner of the room like a bodyguard as the Collins sisters stand somberly at Mia's bedside looking down at her lifeless body. The youngest sister, Tracy, looks the most distraught and touches Mia's hand.

TRACY
(Whispering) Please wake up.

MIA (V.O.)
Guilt... it's a powerful thing... it will
haunt you... especially if you deserve it.

INT. SCHOOL HALLWAY — DAY

The video that the Collins sisters were watching in the waiting room has come to life in
this flashback.

CHAOS... students everywhere... pointing and
laughing... at Mia who is dressed very differ-
ently than every other girl in the hallway. Where
they wear TIGHT and SHORT and Mia wears BAGGY
and LONG.

Mia hurries down the hallway as female voices
call to her.

FEMALE VOICE 1 (O.C.)
Excuse me, Sir... can you tell me where you
got your outfit? I wanna get it for my Dad.

The students laugh again.

FEMALE VOICE 2 (O.C.)
Everything but the shoes because... what
are those?!?!

Mia stops and turns around as the students erupt
with laughter again.

MIA
Why?

                    FEMALE VOICE 3 (O.C.)
     Wait, y'all! It's Mia. Sorry, Mia. We should
     have known it was you... by your smell.

     (Beat) Wooo!

                         MIA
     Are you done?

Mia peers sadly down the hallway at her tormen-
tors as the female voices are revealed to be...
the COLLINS SISTERS!

INT. HOSPITAL — ICU — CONTINUOUS

Tasha moves toward Mia's head and whispers into
her ear.

                        TASHA
       We didn't mean those things we said.

Stephanie touches Mia's leg.

                      STEPHANIE
     Yeah... we're sorry.

                      MIA (V.O.)
     I can't with this...

Once of the machines hooked up to Mia begins to
beep... startling everyone in the room... especially Tracy who runs out crying.

                       TRACY
       It's our fault if she dies!

Tasha and Stephanie rush out of the room after
Tracy as Tina Parker enters.

Tina doesn't even make it to Mia's bed before she breaks down in tears.

Tina stands at a distance... just staring at Mia... tears streaming down her face.

                    TINA
    Why... Mia? You know you could always talk
    to me.

                    MIA (V.O.)
    You're not innocent in this.

                    TINA
    Did I do something? (Beat)

    Did Kevin?

EXT. HOSPITAL PARKING LOT — CONTINUOUS

The crowd in the parking lot has grown and Shannon is interacting with some of the support-ers... off the record.

At the moment, Shannon is in conversation with Kevin Parker.

                    KEVIN
    Linda and my wife, Tina, thought she was
    dead but I got in there and took her pulse
    and... Thank God... she was still alive.

                    SHANNON
    What were you thinking when you saw her
    laying there in all that blood?

                    KEVIN
    Please don't be dead. I hope she survives.
    She's really talented and has a lot to offer
    the world.

                    SHANNON
What kind of talent?

                    KEVIN
(Beaming)

Mia can blow... she is a good singer.

(Beat)

But she's shy. She will only sing when she
knows nobody is around.

Kevin seems tickled by his statement but Shannon
looks at him curiously.

                    SHANNON
(Inquisitively)

So... how is it that you know she can sing?

Kevin's smile immediately disappears. The question obviously caught him off guard and he seems
unsure of how to answer the question... ini-
tially. He quickly recovers and with a smirk,
he answers.

                    KEVIN
Really thin walls.

                    SHANNON
So, you live in the same complex as
Mia's family?

                    KEVIN
Yup. We were there before they moved in.
Tina and Mia got close over the years...
she's like family.

Shannon listens as Kevin talks... she is
making mental notes.

INT. HOSPITAL — ICU — CONTINUOUS

Tina is now right next to Mia's bed... talking one moment... sobbing the next.

                    TINA
    You are like family to me and I will
    never forgive myself if you don't make it
    through this.

                  MIA (V.O.)
    My family has a strange way of showing love
    and... You fit right in.

                    TINA
    I should have done something, my sweet Mia.
    I'm sorry. I'm so sorry.

    Tina gently takes Mia's hand.

                 TINA (CONT'D)
    I hope you can hear me... because I need you
    to know how sorry I am.

Suddenly, Mia's heart monitor starts beeping... startling Tina. John rushes to Mia's side and ushers Tina aside and takes Mia's hand.

As Tina looks on terrified, a team of nurses rush into the room.

                    NURSE
    She's coding!

John rubs Mia's head as he holds her hand.

The nurse is about to tell John to move out of the way but as suddenly as the monitor started beeping... it stops. Was it John's touch?

The Nurse performs an exam on Mia and looks at the readings on her monitors.

                    NURSE (CONT'D)
    Sometimes coma patients respond when they
    hear familiar voices. And they all respond
    in different ways. Maybe this is Mia's way
    of letting us know that she can hear us.

Tina smiles as she hears this but John looks concerned.

EXT. HOSPITAL PARKING LOT — LATER

Shannon is still talking to multiple people in the crowd... closely listening to each of their stories as her reporter's gut is in full gear.

MONTAGE OF QUICK CONVERSATIONS:

Shannon stands in front of an extremely thin, unhealthy looking woman who is talking.

                    THIN WOMAN
    I'm here to support Linda. She and I go
    way back.
    (Gravelly cough)
    She's always been a good mother to her daughter
    so I don't know how this could happen.

NEXT CONVERSATION

Shannon listens attentively to a purposely well-dressed LATIN WOMAN who speaks with concern.

LATIN WOMAN

I'm Mia's guidance counselor, Lilia Gomez,
and I noticed a distinct change in her about
a year or so ago.

SHANNON

How did she change?

LILIA

She completely withdrew from all social
activities and she seemed to go into a
depression. Some girls go through this as
they move into womanhood but with Mia...
something didn't seem right.

Shannon nods her head with understanding.

SHANNON

Thank you, Ms. Gomez, for sharing. This
is the first bit of information that makes
sense in all of this.

LILIA

I care about all of my students and Mia...
I just hope she survives.

NEXT CONVERSATION

Shannon is far from the crowd... intentionally...
as she speaks with a petite AFRICAN AMERICAN
WOMAN who obviously doesn't want anyone to know
she's there.

AFRICAN AMERICAN WOMAN

No cameras and no recording devices, right?

Shannon nods.

> AFRICAN AMERICAN WOMAN (CONT'D)
> Not many people know this but... this isn't
> the first time Mia tried to kill herself.

Shannon leans in... She is all ears!

> AFRICAN AMERICAN WOMAN (CONT'D)
> I work in the nurse's office at Washington
> high school and one day I saw the nurse
> bandaging Mia's wrist.
> (Beat)
> When I asked the nurse about it she said she
> couldn't share but... I knew...

> SHANNON
> So people knew that Mia was unhappy?

> AFRICAN AMERICAN WOMAN
> Yes. But that's not it. Mia's file in the
> nurse's office indicates that there is
> evidence of sexual abuse.

Shannon becomes visibly saddened.

> SHANNON
> And obviously, no one has done anything
> to help this poor young girl. Well... I'm
> going to help her by telling her story.
> (MORE)
> SHANNON (CONT'D)
> (beat)
> Thank you for being brave enough to speak up.

> AFRICAN AMERICAN WOMAN
> I want to help but I don't want any trouble
> so please don't mention me.

                    SHANNON
     You have my word.

The woman looks around to make sure no one is
around or can see her then... she hurries away.

END MONTAGE OF QUICK CONVERSATIONS:

INT. HOSPITAL — ICU — LATER

John peers through the window watching as Miss
Clarita is in the room with Mia.

In the room, Miss Clarita keeps her distance from
Mia and is noticeably emotionally detached.

                    MISS CLARITA
     I know we weren't close but I hope you didn't
     do this because you thought I hated you.
     (Beat)
     I didn't. It was your Mother who just showed
     up with you after all those years.

BEGIN FLASHBACK

EXT. SMALL HOUSE — DAY

A MUCH younger Linda walks up the steps with a
little girl (3 or 4) toward a BARRED front door.
Linda knocks on the door and waits nervously.

The door opens and Miss Clarita stands there. She
should look a lot younger but she doesn't. Same
hairdo... same type of clothes... same scowl.

LINDA
Hey, Mom. This is my daughter, Mia.

Miss Clarita doesn't respond. She just stares...

END FLASHBACK

INT. HOSPITAL — ICU — CONTINUOUS

MISS CLARITA
She robbed me of those years. And I was
angry at her... not you.

MIA (V.O.)
So that's why you treated me like I didn't
exist? Yeah... makes sense.

BEGIN FLASHBACK

INT. SMALL HOUSE — DAY

Young Mia (7 or 8) is in a house full of
people... she is watching sadly as Miss
Clarita is laughing and playing with young
girls her age... and no one even notices her.

END FLASHBACK

INT. HOSPITAL — ICU — CONTINUOUS

MISS CLARITA

As you got older, I tried to get closer to you
but...

BEGIN FLASHBACK

INT. SCHOOL AUDITORIUM — NIGHT

Mia (12 or 13) is on stage receiving a trophy and looking into the audience but not seeing anyone there to support her.

At the back of the auditorium... in the doorway stands Miss Clarita. She starts to walk toward the front of the auditorium but shakes her head, turns around, and leaves without letting Mia know she was there.

END FLASHBACK

INT. HOSPITAL — ICU — CONTINUOUS

MISS CLARITA
I guess too much time passed and you didn't want to know me.

MIA (V.O.)
Is that what you want to believe to make yourself feel better?

John enters the room with another man, ALEXANDER BERG, 50's. Mr. Berg looks like a boss... dressed in a HIGH DOLLAR SUIT... his air of confidence completely makes up for his below average physical stature.

JOHN
Miss Clarita... Can Mr. Berg visit with Mia? He's on a tight schedule.

Miss Clarita looks at John and exits the room without even acknowledging Mr. Berg.

John approaches Mia's bed and whispers in her ear.

                    JOHN (CONT'D)
     Mia... my boss, Mr. Berg, wants to talk
     to you.

Mr. Berg approaches Mia's bed and John steps back.

                    MR. BERG
     Hey, Mia. It's Mr. Alex. I was just telling
     John what I remember of you as a little girl.
     Your mother would bring you to the shelter
     and you were always smiling and singing.

BEGIN FLASHBACK

INT. HOMELESS SHELTER — DAY

Young Mia (7 or 8) sings as she helps Linda pack lunches. Mr. Berg enters the room.

                    MIA
     (Smiling) Hey, Mr. Alex!

Mr. Berg gives Mia a "high five" and pulls Linda into another room with him.

When Linda and Mr. Berg return, Linda is somber. Mr. Berg smiles at Mia, gives her another "high five," and exits the room.

END FLASHBACK

INT. HOSPITAL — ICU — CONTINUOUS

> MR. BERG
> As I watched you grow up, I told your Mother that you were a special young woman and that I wanted to make sure you get to use your talents.
>
> (Frowns)
>
> I had no idea you were in so much pain.

Mr. Berg looks back at John who shakes his head.

> MR. BERG (CONT'D)
> What happened? I thought you were okay.
>
> (Beat)
>
> I wish you would have come and talked to me if you were having problems.

> MIA (V.O.)
> (Sarcastic laugh)
>
> Drugs were not the answer to my problems, Mr. Alex.

> MR. BERG
> I will be praying for your full recovery.

Mr. Berg bends down and kisses Mia on the forehead. Then he turns and steps toward John who walks him out of the room.

As they exit, Linda enters. Mr. Berg touches Linda on the shoulder and John gives her a peck on the lips.

Linda pulls up a chair next to Mia's bed and sits down.

                          LINDA

Do you remember the time we were in line to
buy tickets to see Alicia Keys? You woke me
up so early because you wanted to be first
in line. But you got the time wrong and when
we got there... it was sold out.

Linda's words dissolve into a flashback.

EXT. HOUSE OF BLUES — DAY

Linda and a younger Mia (12 or 13) hustle to the
box office window.

                          MIA

(Excitedly)

See! I told you we would be first!

Mia gets to the window and eagerly makes
her request.

                      MIA (CONT'D)
Two tickets to the Alicia Keys concert.

                      TICKET AGENT
I'm sorry, young lady, the concert is
already sold out.

                          MIA
But the tickets just went on sale at
12:00 noon.

                      TICKET AGENT
Actually, it was 12:00 am.

Mia is devastated.

                    TICKET AGENT (CONT'D)
Maybe   you   can   find   someone   that   is
re-selling them.

Linda steps to the window and speaks in an
uncharacteristically sweet tone.

                         LINDA
Listen... this is my daughter's favorite
artist. Are you sure there aren't some
special tickets somewhere? I'm willing to
pay for them.

Linda flashes the male ticket agent a smile and
winks at him.

                    TICKET AGENT
I'm   sorry,   Ma'am.   There   are   no   more
tickets available.

Linda's sweet demeanor changes immediately. She
gets closer to the window and talks low so Mia
can't hear her.

                         LINDA
You live in Mr. Berg's neighborhood, right?

The Ticket Agent nods.

                    LINDA (CONT'D)
Well, this is Mr. Berg's niece and if he
finds out she's sad... he won't be happy.
So... I suggest you find some tickets.
    (Beat) Are we good?

The Ticket Agent nods.

Linda backs away from the window and immediately resumes smiling.

LINDA (CONT'D)
Me-Me... Great news... turns out there is another way to get tickets. All you have to do is sing your favorite Alicia Keys song. If you know all the words... you get the tickets.

Mia smiles as she looks at the Ticket Agent who nods his head.

LINDA (CONT'D)
Okay, Baby... sing.

Mia begins to sing "Girl on Fire." Before Mia finishes, Linda claps.

LINDA (CONT'D)
That's my girl! Amazing, Me-Me! So talented.
(To Ticket Agent) Right?!

TICKET AGENT
(Clapping) Amazing.

The Ticket Agent hands two tickets to Mia.

TICKET AGENT (CONT'D)
Congratulations.

MIA
Thank you so much!

Linda nods at the Ticket Agent. As Mia turns to walk away, Linda flashes a threatening smile at the Ticket Agent.

END FLASHBACK

INT. HOSPITAL — ICU — NIGHT

                    LINDA
You really are talented. I hope I didn't screw you up so much that you don't get to use it.

             MIA (V.O.)
You sound sincere but then again... I've heard this before.

Linda's moment with Mia is interrupted as a team of nurses come in to perform their routine examinations.

While the nurses are working on Mia, John strolls into the room with balloons and flowers. He walks over to Linda and gives her exaggerated kiss... for show.

                  JOHN
How you holding up, Sweetie? You should go home and sleep in our comfortable bed.

                  LINDA
That sounds good.

Linda begins to gather her things.

              HEAD NURSE
Mr. Daniels, flowers are not allowed in the ICU.

                  JOHN
(Smiling)

These aren't for the room... they're for you and your team for all that you are doing for Mia.

(Beat)

I wanted to make sure you all know how much we appreciate you.

All of the nurses smile.

> HEAD NURSE
> Aren't you just so sweet?

John doesn't respond but he flashes a seductive smile at the Head Nurse... who blushes.

> MIA (V.O.)
> You have them fooled just like you had me...
> (Scoffs) And Linda.

BEGIN FLASHBACK

INT. APARTMENT — LIVING ROOM — EVENING

Linda is sitting on the couch, all dressed up, but she looks unhappy. Mia (14) comes into the living room and sees her mother.

> MIA
> What are you still doing here? I figured you'd be halfway through dinner with John by now.

Linda's response almost feels like she's covering for John.

                    LINDA

Oh... he said something came up at work that
he had to take care of. He'll be here soon.

                    MIA

Didn't this happen a couple of times last
week too?

                    LINDA

He's busy, okay?

                    MIA

Okay. I just don't want you to get hurt.

                    LINDA

(Smiling)

That's sweet of you. But I'm a big girl.
I'll be okay.

Someone knocks on the door and Linda smiles.
She goes to open it and John is standing there
with roses.

                    JOHN

Sorry. I'm so late.

Mia observes the scene and sees her mother swoon.

                    MIA

(To John) Nice save.

                    LINDA

   Mia!

John laughs.

                    JOHN

No... I deserve it. But I will make it up
to you. I promise.

John helps Linda put on her coat and as they walk out, John turns back to Mia.

                    JOHN (CONT'D)
     Good night, Mia.

John winks at Mia and strolls out the door.

END FLASHBACK

EXT. HOSPITAL PARKING LOT — NIGHT

The crowd has grown even bigger. There are lit candles and handmade signs of encouragement for Mia, her family, and her community.

The camera is rolling as David lines up a shot of Shannon interviewing MR. CHARLES JAY, 40's, tall, slender, soft- spoken, and definitely nervous to be speaking into the camera.

                    SHANNON
     Good evening, Shannon Price, News Nine here
     at a candlelight vigil for Mia Reynolds, the
     young woman who was found shot yesterday in
     her apartment.
     (Beat)
     I'm standing with Mr. Charles Jay, a business
     owner in Mia's community.
     Can you tell us something about the victim
     from your perspective?
                    MR. JAY
     I only saw Mia when she would come into my
     store. She was always respectful and she
     never stole nothing. She's a good kid.

SHANNON
(Semi-sarcastically) Thank you, Mr. Jay.

As Mr. Jay walks away Shannon spots Mr. Berg coming out of the hospital and hurriedly crosses to him... David following closely.

Shannon catches up to Mr. Berg and bombards him with questions.

SHANNON (CONT'D)
Mr. Alexander Berg. Shannon Price, News Nine.

Mr. Berg does his best to keep a smile on his face but you can tell that he is not pleased to see Shannon.

MR. BERG
Of course, Ms. Price. What can I do for you?

SHANNON
Do you know Mia Reynolds?

MR. BERG
That's really none of your business but... as a matter of fact I do.

SHANNON
Reporting the news is my business. And you know that when something seems shady, I'm going to question it.

MR. BERG
Your reporter's gut again, Ms. Price?

(Almost threatening)

That got you in trouble in the past. But I'm sure you learned from that experience.

Shannon doesn't respond.

                    MR. BERG (CONT'D)
Well... so you don't jump to conclusions...
I'm here because I support my community and
this tragedy hit close to home.

(Devilish smile)

Nothing sinister or "shady" here, Ms. Price.

Shannon forces a smile.

                    SHANNON
That's good to know. Thank you, Mr. Berg.
Have a good night.

                    MR. BERG
You as well, Ms. Price.

Mr. Berg shakes his head and struts away. Shannon
watches as Mr. Berg leaves and sees that he and
Mr. Jay and Mike Murphy all nod to each other.

David peers at Shannon and takes a deep exasper-
ated breath.

                    DAVID
You need to leave that man alone. Berg
hasn't always been an upstanding business
man, you know? Don't press this one.

Shannon doesn't respond... she just continues
to watch Mr. Berg until he disappears from
her sight.

EXT. APARTMENT COMPLEX COURTYARD — DAY

Shannon walks through the red brick courtyard toward the Daniels' apartment when something catches her eye. It's the reflection of the

sun from a cellphone. MIA'S CELLPHONE (although Shannon doesn't know it yet).

Shannon picks up the cellphone and continues toward the Daniel's apartment. She pauses before she knocks on the door because she hears Linda crying.

Shannon hears the crying stop abruptly and she quickly knocks on the door... no answer.

Shannon knocks again... no answer. Concerned... Shannon knocks and calls to Linda.

                    SHANNON
    Mrs. Daniels! Mrs. Daniels... are you okay?

The door opens suddenly and Linda stands there looking dazed... under the influence of something strong.

                  SHANNON (CONT'D)
    Mrs. Daniels? I'm Shannon Price. Are
    you okay?

                    LINDA
    Do I look okay, News lady?

Shannon doesn't respond as she studies Linda whose eyes are glassy.

                  LINDA (CONT'D)
    That's not very observant of you as
    a reporter.

Shannon ignores the comment and enter the apartment.

INT. APARTMENT — CONTINUOUS

                    SHANNON
    You weren't at the hospital this morning.

                    LINDA
    (Defensively)

    So that makes me a bad mother?

Shannon is surprised by/curious of
Linda's response.

                    SHANNON
    No, Mrs. Daniels... I just want to ask you
    some questions.

                    LINDA
    Let me ask you a question... do you have
    children, Ms. Price?

This question triggers a sadness in Shannon.

                    SHANNON
    No... I lost my only child at birth.

                    LINDA
    Sorry to hear that. No mother should ever
    have to bury her child.

Shannon looks away but doesn't respond.

                    LINDA (CONT'D)
    So you understand how difficult this time is
    for me, right?

Shannon nods.

                    LINDA (CONT'D)
Then tell me what kind of questions you
would want to answer after you experienced
your tragedy, Ms.

Price?

                    SHANNON
(Apologetically)

I am truly sorry, Mrs. Daniels. I do not mean
to be insensitive in this difficult time.

(MORE)

                SHANNON (CONT'D)
I was just hoping to be able to share
some bright spots in Mia's life for all
those out there who have been supporting
your daughter.

                    LINDA
Bright spots?

(Sarcastic smirk) Bright spots?

(Incredulously)

How many bright spots make you want to
kill yourself?

(Beat) Huh?!?!

Shannon just listens as Linda starts to
break down.

                    LINDA (CONT'D)
Oh... maybe growing up without a father?
Or... having your family turn their backs
on you?

Linda's face begins to stream tears.

> LINDA (CONT'D)
> Or what about having an alcoholic for
> a mother?
>
> (Beat)
>
> Are those the bright spots you're
> talking about?

Linda becomes even more downcast as something
dawns on her...

> LINDA (CONT'D)
> Like mother like daughter, I guess.
>
> With that... Linda passes out on the couch.

Shannon checks to make sure Linda is okay and...
She is. The reporter in Shannon comes out and she
begins to walk through the apartment. Heading
first to the back bedroom where the caution tape
is still up.

INT. APARTMENT — BEDROOM 2 — CONTINUOUS

Shannon studies the crime scene. As she moves
forward, the scene replays... each step that
Mia took... but this time... it's not Mia... it
is SHANNON!

Shannon sees the smashed PHOTO of LINDA and JOHN
on the floor and sees herself throwing it to
the ground.

Shannon walks to the closet and looks down at the
carpet still stained with blood. She closes her
eyes and imagines Mia holding the gun to hear
head in the closet.

Suddenly... BANG!!! The room briefly lights up from the gun blast!!!

Shannon is a bit shaken and hurries out of that room and into...

INT. APARTMENT — BEDROOM 1 — CONTINUOUS

Shannon enters Mia's room and studies it closely. She sees that items are missing from the shelf of trophies. She sees an empty space between two desk speakers where obviously some kind of music player used to be and... The scratch pad that Mia scribbled on.

Shannon picks up the scratch pad and reads what is written on the note, "It's time for the pain to end. Soon, the truth will come out."

Shannon folds up the note, puts it in her pocket, and rushes out of the room and out of the apartment.

EXT. HOSPITAL PARKING LOT — LATER

Shannon is back at her post as the crowd con-tinues to grow with supporters. Paul Kramer approaches Shannon.

> PASTOR KRAMER
> Ms. Price, the church is having a prayer night tonight. Can you let your viewers know?

> SHANNON
> Is your church big enough to hold all 20 of my viewers?

Shannon and Pastor Kramer share a chuckle. But then Pastor Kramer becomes sorrowful.

                    PASTOR KRAMER
    It's still hard to believe why we're here.
    Mia used to make me and Peyton laugh all
    the time when she first started coming to
    our house.

BEGIN FLASHBACK

INT. KRAMER HOUSE — DAY

Slightly younger Mia and PK sit at the dining room table in the Kramer's small and meager but comfortable house. Both girls have their noses buried in books.

                    PK
    Who needs algebra 2 anyway? I mean... are we
    really going to need use imaginary numbers?

                    MIA
    Girls in my neighborhood use imaginary
    numbers all the time.

PK peers at Mia curiously.

                    PK
    What you mean, girl?

                    MIA
    When a guy you don't like asks you for your
    number...
    (Smiling)
    You give him what?

PK laughs out loud...

                    PK
An imaginary number.

                    MIA
Exactly! (310) 987-6543.

Both girls laugh heartily.

                    PK
You got jokes... but I guess you can when
you ace every math test.

Pastor Kramer enters and joins in.

               PASTOR KRAMER
Did I hear you girls talking about
imaginary numbers?

                    MIA
Yes, Sir.

               PASTOR KRAMER
(Smiles)
Do you know what I said to pi?

Mia smiles but doesn't respond.

                    PK
No, Dad... what?

               PASTOR KRAMER
Be rational. Ha!

Pastor Kramer laughs... he is so pleased with himself.

                    MIA
So... what did pi say to i?

PK and Pastor Kramer stare blankly at each other. Mia tries to contain her smile but she can't.

                 MIA (CONT'D)
     Get real...

Mia lets out a belly laugh as PK shakes her head and smiles at Mia. Pastor Kramer laughs too.

                PASTOR KRAMER
     Good one, Mia! I'll have to use that one.
     (Looks at his watch)
     Well, I don't want to intrude any more than I already have so, I'm going to go to my meeting.
     (Beat)
     You girls have a good time studying... or whatever you call this.

Pastor Kramer gently pulls PK out of her chair and gives her a tight embrace and peck on the cheek.

              PASTOR KRAMER (CONT'D)
     Love you, Princess.
                    PK
     (Smiling)
     Love you too, Daddy.

Pastor Kramer crosses to Mia and she stands up.

PASTOR KRAMER
Thank you for studying with my girl.

Pastor Kramer gives Mia a respectful SIDE HUG and it looks like that catches her off-guard.

PASTOR KRAMER (CONT'D)
You're certainly a good influence on her grades.

Pastor Kramer smiles subtly at PK and exits.

PK
Yeah, Mia... thanks to you, I somehow got a B on our last test.

MIA
Come on PK, give yourself some credit.

PK
Really? Says the girl who covers up her amazing body?

MIA
As a Pastor's Kid... you of all people should respect modesty, PK.

PK
Of course I do but... we ain't nuns, girl.

PK laughs but Mia remains serious.

PK (CONT'D)
What's wrong, Mia?

Mia just stares at PK...

END FLASHBACK

EXT. HOSPITAL PARKING LOT — CONTINUOUS

Pastor Kramer continues to share his recollection with Shannon.

> PASTOR KRAMER
> Mia was so full of life. Then... she changed.
> My daughter told me that Mia confided in her
> and shared a lot of private details.
> (Somberly)
> I hope she doesn't feel guilty for
> not sharing.

> SHANNON
> Do you have any idea what Mia shared with
> your daughter?

> PASTOR KRAMER
> PK is a good friend and she would never
> betray a friend's trust... not even to
> her Dad.

> SHANNON
> I get that. And I respect it. (Beat)
> But I'm sensing that you, like me, know
> that something is definitely missing from
> this picture of why Mia would do this.

Pastor Kramer nods his head in agreement.

> SHANNON (CONT'D)
> Soon, the truth will come out.

Shannon smiles and nods to herself as she puts her hand in her pocket and pulls out Mia's note.

INT. HOSPITAL — ICU — NIGHT

Linda and John sit quietly in chairs on opposite sides of Mia's bed... the tension is obvious as they sit in complete silence... the only sound heard is the machine that is breathing for Mia.

                    LINDA
    (Agitatedly)
    What do you really want, John?

                    MIA (V.O.)
    Finally! A backbone.

                    JOHN
    What do you mean?

                    LINDA
    You know what I mean. (Beat)
    I see the way you look at her.

John remains silent... peering at Linda intensely.

                    LINDA (CONT'D)
    Do you want her -?

John coughs... interrupting Linda's thought.

                    LINDA (CONT'D)
    Do you want her to live... or die? Because...
    you've never treated her like a daughter.

John drops his defensive posture and sheds a half smile.

                    JOHN

Of course I want Mia to live! Yes, we may
have a unique relationship but she's your
little girl. I think I just came into your
lives too late to be a father but... that
doesn't mean I don't care about her...
because I do.

                    LINDA

How can you even say that? You never spent
any time with us... me and her. It was
always just me.

(Beat)

You were always working at night when she
was home and here when she was at school.

John is starting to get upset but he keeps
his cool.

                    JOHN

I work at night because that's what's
needed. And... I can make more money this
way. But you never complained about that.

(Beat) Why now?

                    LINDA

It's not about the money, John. I am tired of
fighting over money. I just want my husband
but... you seem to want to be somewhere else.

                    JOHN

Where is this coming from?

                    LINDA

I'm starting to piece some things together.

                  MIA (V.O.)

It's about time!

John regains his defensive posture and tries to deflect the onslaught.

                    JOHN
I think being here so much is doing something to you.

                    LINDA
You know what else does something to you?

(MORE)

                    LINDA (CONT'D)
(Beat)

Being home every night, wondering what your husband is doing.

(Beat)

I made some very bad decisions because of it... that I'll regret for the rest of my life.

                    JOHN
So, you're trying to blame me because you fell off the wagon?

                    LINDA
(Scoffs)

I wish that was all it was. (Downcast)

Mia is paying for my sins.

                    MIA (V.O.)
Where was this clarity when it mattered? It's too late to come to Jesus now.

BEGIN FLASHBACK

EXT. APARTMENT COMPLEX COURTYARD — NIGHT

A group of women including Tina Parker, Brooke Hill, and Linda stand around talking.

Mike Murphy approaches the group still wearing his BLUE MAILMAN UNIFORM and stops next to Linda who seems fidgety.

> MIKE
> Got your text. I'll take a look at your toilet since John isn't home.

> LINDA
> (Overly appreciative) Thank you so much, Mike!

Linda leads Mike to her apartment.

INT. APARTMENT — CONTINUOUS

As they enter the apartment, Mike puts something in Linda's hand and then she shows Mike to the bathroom.

Linda heads back to the door and calls to Mike.

> LINDA
> I'll be back later. Please, just lock the door when you're done.

> MIKE
> All good. You have a good night.

As Linda walks toward the door, she opens her hand and sees two ONE HUNDRED DOLLAR BILLS and sheds a kind of sad smile.

INT. MIA'S ROOM — MOMENTS LATER

Mia is in her bed... visibly sad and withdrawn as Mike Murphy zips up his pants, grabs his blue uniform jacket, and walks out of her room.

END FLASHBACK

INT. HOSPITAL — ICU — CONTINUOUS

> MIA (V.O.)
> I used to think... "She doesn't know."
> (Beat)
> Because... how could you let this happen to your daughter if you knew?

> INT. MIA'S ROOM — NIGHT
> Mia is in her bed... tears streaming down her face as another random nameless man puts on his pants and walks out her of her room.

> MIA (V.O.)
> There were so many. How could she not know?

> INT. MIA'S ROOM — NIGHT
> Mia is in her bed... head buried under the covers... trying to hide from what just happened... as Mr. Jay walks out of her room.

> MIA (V.O.)
> At first... I thought I was going to die. It hurt so much. And not just... physically.

> MIA (V.O.)
> Was something wrong with me?

INT. MIA'S ROOM — NIGHT

Mia is laying in her bed... emotionless looking up at the ceiling... as another man from her neighborhood gazes at Mia while he buttons up his shirt. Mia never looks his way so he turns and walks out of her room.

                    MIA (V.O.)
Did I do something to make these men think I wanted this?

(Beat)

Was it the way I dressed? (Beat)

Did I smell too good to them?

INT. MIA'S ROOM — NIGHT

Mia is sitting up in her bed... clutching the sheets with both hands near her chin... sadly shaking her head as she watches well-built STEVE HILL, 40's, the salt-and-pepper bearded, handsome husband of Brooke Hill walk out of her room.

As Steve opens the door, Mia's eyes get big with shock... and she immediately begins to cry and sob.

From Mia's POV, we see Steve giving money to... LINDA.

INT. HOSPITAL — ICU — CONTINUOUS

Suddenly, Mia's heart monitor begins to beep and the numbers climb.

                    MIA (V.O.)
Of course she knew. (Dejected)

> She let this happen to me so she could get
> high. (Or feed her habit)

Immediately, a team of nurses rush in and begin
to work on Mia as Linda and John look on... fear-
ing that this could be it for Mia.

From Linda's POV the scene moves in slow motion
as inaudible chatter between the team of nurses
can be heard as they scramble to try to save Mia.

                    MIA (V.O.)
        And those men... those disgusting men...
        what was their excuse?

After a few tense moments... the nurses are able
to get Mia's monitors to stop beeping and return
to normal.

Linda appears to be relieved but John remains
emotionless as he stares at Mia.

INT. HOSPITAL WAITING ROOM — CONTINUOUS

The waiting room is not as crowded as it was on
the night Mia was originally brought in but there
are still a fair number of people waiting to hear
an update on Mia's condition.

PK, Brooke Hill, Tina Parker, and surprisingly...
Tracy Collins are among the neighbors and friends
who sit nervously anxiously waiting.

Shannon enters the waiting room alone and as
discreetly as possible as to not call a lot of

attention to herself. She scans the room and goes directly to PK.

> SHANNON
> Hey PK, I'm Shannon.

PK is shocked that Shannon knows her name and it is evident by the expression on her face.

> SHANNON (CONT'D)
> I've been speaking with your father outside at the vigil and he told me that you and Mia were very close.

> PK
> Mia is my girl. She was the first friend I made when me and my family moved here.

> SHANNON
> When was that?

> PK
> A little more than a year ago.

> SHANNON
> In the time you've known Mia, how would you characterize her personality?
> (Beat)
> Was she happy? Depressed? Up and down?

> PK
> When I first met Mia, I saw this smart, talented, and compassionate person.

BEGIN FLASHBACK

EXT. BACKYARD — DAY

15 year old PK and Mia sit at a table preparing for a science experiment. Mia is doing most of the work as PK hands her items. Both girls are dressed modestly but Mia, as usual, has taken it to another level by wearing clothes that are extremely unflattering to her body.

Mia is smiling and singing a Beyonce song... and she sounds good... so good that PK stops helping her and just listens.

PK is broken out of her trance by the sound of a barking dog fast approaching.

Before they know it, the dog is on the table and their set up gets scattered everywhere.

P.K's little brother, TOMMY KRAMER, 10, a skinny, redhead with freckles races to catch up with the dog.

                    PK
     (Sternly)
     D-O-G! Get down!

Tommy approaches and PK lays into him.

               PK (CONT'D)
     Tommy! Didn't I tell you not to let D-O-G
     out here? Now, look what he did! You're 10!
     You shouldn't be this useless!

Tommy is obviously hurt and walks away...
crushed. Mia sees this and looks sad herself.

                    MIA
          He didn't mean it, PK.

                    PK
He's always doing stuff like this.

                    MIA
Yeah but... he's your little brother. I'm
sure he looks up to you and I know that
hurt him.

(MORE)

               MIA (CONT'D)
(Downcast)

I wish I had a sibling.

                    PK
You say that because you don't have one
who's always messing things up for you.

                    MIA
    We can fix this experiment, PK. (beat)
But you can't fix the damage done by family.

PK stares at Mia as she ponders her words.

                    PK
You are something else, Mia.

PK smiles at Mia and then gets up and goes
to Tommy.

Mia watches from a distance as PK says something
to Tommy and then moves in to embrace him.

Mia smiles as PK and Tommy embrace.

END FLASHBACK

INT. HOSPITAL WAITING ROOM — CONTINUOUS

Shannon listens intently as PK continues
her story.

> PK
>
> It wasn't until she really opened up to me
> that I knew how tough her life had been. She
> just didn't show it.

> SHANNON
>
> What kind of things did she share with you?

> PK
>
> I don't think I should be sharing her personal
> business... especially with a reporter.

> SHANNON
>
> I understand your concern but please know
> that I am not trying to find this out as a
> reporter... but as someone who has been
> through something similar.

PK peers skeptically at Shannon.

> SHANNON (CONT'D)
>
> I'm going to share something with you that
> not many people know.

PK nods at Shannon.

> SHANNON (CONT'D)
>
> When I was Mia's age, I got pregnant and lost
> my baby. For a long time I was depressed.

And one night... I took some pills. A lot of pills.

P.K's skepticism dissolves from her face and she looks at Shannon with a compassionate half smile.

                    PK
I'm sorry to hear that. I can't imagine.

                    SHANNON
I'm just trying to put the pieces together to find out why Mia did this. And... I want to help inform people so that no other young person feels like this is their only choice... because it's not.

(Beat)

I got another chance. And I hope that Mia does too.

PK's mood becomes melancholy. Shannon notices.

                    SHANNON (CONT'D)
You do have hope, right? I know your Father does.

                    PK
It's no that... (Beat)

I feel like I let Mia down.

                    SHANNON
What do you mean?

                    PK
I wasn't there for her when she needed me.

                    SHANNON
What did she need?

                         PK
She opened up to me about her Mother's
addiction... and that she got pregnant and
had an abortion just before we met. And
about a man she loved.

As PK is talking, she notices that Linda and John
are about to enter the waiting room and she immediately stops talking.

Shannon notices.

                      SHANNON
Did she tell you who the man is?

PK remains quiet as she looks at John. Shannon
notices and looks on curiously.

                         PK
(Nervously)
No... She didn't get a chance to.

John takes hold of Linda's hand, puts on his
charismatic smile, and they walk to the center of
the waiting room.

                       JOHN
Hey, everybody, please listen up. (Smiling
and nodding)

First... Linda and I would like to thank
all of the family, close friends, and even
hospital staff for all of your support
through this incredibly difficult situation.

John's charm and command of the room is undeni-
able... the whole waiting room comes to a halt
once he begins to talk.

                    JOHN (CONT'D)
Trust me... we know that waiting is the
hardest part of all of this.

So... we want to give you an update on
Mia's condition.

Almost in perfect synchronization... everyone in
the waiting room sits up and focuses on John in
anticipation of what's coming.

                    JOHN (CONT'D)
Although Mia has made it this far... she is
far from being out of the woods. But she's a
fighter and we are hoping that she continues
to fight.

John pauses to plant a kiss on Linda's forehead... for the "theatrics" of it all.

                    JOHN (CONT'D)
I know many of you are here still waiting to
be able to say your "good-byes" but Mia's
body has gone through a lot today and she
needs her rest. So, we're asking that you
please come back tomorrow.

Some of the people in the waiting room appear
to be disappointed by John's request. John sees
this...

                    JOHN (CONT'D)
Please don't be disappointed... we want
everyone to get a chance to see her and
talk to her but right now... your continued

prayers are the best thing for Mia at this point in time.

As the people begin to get up and leave the room, Shannon approaches John and Linda.

>   SHANNON
> Hello, Mr. and Mrs. Daniels.

>   LINDA
> Hello, Ms. Price.

>   JOHN
> (Curiously)
> You two know each other?

>   LINDA
> We do... Ms. Price came to the house to talk to me about doing a story on Mia to get more support for us.

Shannon flashes a quick smile and goes along with Linda's flowery version of their last encounter.

>   SHANNON
> Yes... thank you for your time. I believe the information you provided has raised awareness of the situation.

John looks on suspiciously.

>   JOHN
> What can we do for you now, Ms. Price?

>   SHANNON
> What happened to Mia is a tragedy but... maybe it could have been avoided.

                    JOHN
I'm not following you.

                  SHANNON
I have some personal experience with
attempted suicide and it is my hope that
I will be able to help others not make
that choice.

                    JOHN
And how are you going to do that?

                  SHANNON
By getting to the bottom of why people feel
that suicide is their only choice.

John's relaxed persona tenses up a bit.

                    JOHN
Why do you think Mia "made that choice"?

                  SHANNON
I don't know yet. But I'd like to ask you
and your wife some questions. Just to get a
baseline on who Mia is.

Linda takes a deep breath.

              SHANNON (CONT'D)
I've spoken with some of your neighbors,
friends, and family but... you two must
know her best.

John peers into Linda's eyes and rubs
her shoulders.

                    JOHN
Today has been a long day, Ms. Price, and
my wife needs to get her rest.

John kisses Linda on the lips and...

                    JOHN (CONT'D)
You go home and get some rest. I will see
you in the morning when I get off work.

(Beat)

I will stay and answer some questions for
Ms. Price.

Linda nods.

                    LINDA
Okay. See you in the morning. (To Shannon)

See you next time.

                    SHANNON
(Nodding)

Hope you get the rest you need.

Linda drags herself down the hallway as she is
exhausted. John smiles as he watches her all the
way and when she is out of sight... his smile
immediately disappears and he turns his attention
to Shannon.

                    JOHN
Okay, Ms. Price. What are you really after?
You are a reporter. What's your angle?

Shannon is caught off-guard... a little.

                    SHANNON
Like I said... I just want to help others.
And any information I can gather to paint the
picture of why people do it... is important.

(Beat)

Like the fact that you work nights...

                    JOHN

Yes... I work nights. I am the manager of the South L.A. homeless shelter. Surely, you don't think me working at night to help others get back on their feet is a cause for Mia's bad choice, do you?

                    SHANNON

Do you know how you not being around at night impacted Mia?

                    JOHN

(Irritated)

Do you even know Mia? (Beat)

Because if you did... you would know that she and I had a great relationship. Not like your typical "step" relationship.

                    SHANNON

Well, that's good. So, was she able to talk to you about anything?

                    JOHN

Mia was a very serious girl and she didn't share much but I think she knew she could talk to me about anything.

                    SHANNON

(Probing)

So, how did her pregnancy and subsequent termination affect her?

This catches John completely off-guard... how does she know about that?

                    JOHN
You know, Ms. Price. I think the question
and answer session is over.

Shannon persists.

                    SHANNON
Just one last answer, Mr. Daniels.

John uncharacteristically glares angrily
at Shannon.

                    JOHN
(Sternly)

I said, "We're done."

John turns and storms off as Shannon watches with
a determined look on her face... she is definitely
on a mission now to find out more about John.

    INT. HOSPITAL — ICU — LATER

The team of nurses continue to work on Mia and
monitor her vitals.

                    NURSE
Her vitals have finally reached a safe range.

(Relieved)

She must be thinking happy thoughts.

                    MIA (V.O.)
I had a happy thought once.

BEGIN FLASHBACK

INT. FANCY RESTAURANT — EVENING

Mia is wearing a beautiful black dress and jew-
elry that emphasizes just how exquisite she
looks. Her hair is in an elegant up-do and she is
figuratively glowing as her huge smile lights up
the room.

A TRIO of musicians serenade Mia's table... playing one of her favorite songs by her favorite
artist, Alicia Keys.

Mia looks across the table and smiles widely but
the face of her companion is obscured.

> MIA (V.O.)
> But you aren't the man I thought you were.
> So... fantasy over.

END FLASHBACK

INT. HOSPITAL — ICU — CONTINUOUS

Mia is alone in her dark hospital room as the
last nurse has just turned off the lights and
walked out.

> MIA (V.O.)
> And the reality is... I should have known.
> (Disappointed)
> How could I have been so stupid? (Sure)
> It's who you are.

EXT. HOMELESS SHELTER — DAY

Shannon is alone as she approaches the entrance
of the homeless shelter. She cautiously scans
her surroundings as there are some sketchy folks
hanging around this building.

As Shannon is about to walk through the front
entrance, she hears a voice trying to get
her attention.

                    VOICE
          Over here, Miss Reporter.

Shannon looks around and sees a woman waving for
her to come to her.

Shannon walks toward the woman but the
woman turns and goes behind the building.
Shannon follows.

Shannon catches up with the woman who has stopped
in an alley behind the building. The woman, DEBRA
LOCK, is possibly in her late 30's but the wear
and tear on her body makes her look like she's in
her late 50's. She is fidgety and nervous as she
constantly looks around.

                    SHANNON
          You know who I am?

                    DEBRA
          Everybody knows who you are. Especially
          now...

                    SHANNON
Do you have some information?

                    DEBRA
Do you have some money for information?

                    SHANNON
Look... you came to me. But obviously, you
are wasting my time.

Shannon turns to leave.

                    DEBRA
You came here for something, Miss Reporter.
What you looking for?

Shannon doesn't respond... she walks away.

                DEBRA (CONT'D)
This ain't just no homeless shelter.

Shannon keeps walking.

                DEBRA (CONT'D)
It's a cover for drugs.

Shannon stops in her tracks. She turns back
toward Debra.

                    SHANNON
Where's your evidence?

                    DEBRA
(Sarcastic chuckle)
You think I come here for the chicken
noodle soup?

Debra pulls up her sleeves and holds out her
arms... revealing several track marks.

Now Shannon is all ears.

                    DEBRA (CONT'D)
     You can buy and use drugs here. And nobody
     thinks nothing of it because this is a place
     where they are helping people get back on
     their feet.

Shannon recalls John using the same words.

                    JOHN (V.O.)
     Surely, you don't think me working at night
     to help others get back on their feet is a
     cause for Mia's bad choice, do you?

                    SHANNON
     Do you know the night manager?

                    DEBRA
     I don't but I heard about him. He's no
     good. I think his name is John or something
     like that.

Shannon can't believe what she's hearing.

                    DEBRA (CONT'D)
     But he's the little man... this is
     Berg's operation.

BINGO!!! Now Shannon gets the connection.

                    SHANNON
     And you're not afraid that Berg is going to
     try to harm you for telling me all of this?

                    DEBRA

Honey... Berg would just be speeding up
the inevitable.

(Beat)

(MORE)

                 DEBRA (CONT'D)

Too many needles caught up with me... HIV...
and not the Magic Johnson kind... my time
is just about up. So... I ain't got nothing
to lose.

                   SHANNON

You sure there's nothing you can do?

                    DEBRA

I'm at a homeless shelter... with drugs...
but I can't get those kind of drugs here.

                   SHANNON

(Sincerely)

Thank you for your courage.

                    DEBRA

Somebody has to step up... our neighborhood
deserves better.

Shannon nods and smiles at Debra. As Shannon
turns to walk away, she gets the feeling someone
is watching her so she looks around but doesn't
see anyone.

As Shannon walks away, it is revealed that someone was watching the whole interaction from a
second story window in the shelter but the person's identity is not revealed.

INT. HOSPITAL — ICU — DAY

Mia is alone in the room as the Head
Nurse enters.

> MIA (V.O.)
> (Inhaling)
> Where is that smell coming from?

As the Head Nurse get closer, the smell
gets stronger.

> MIA (V.O.)
> I know that smell.

BEGIN FLASHBACK

INT. MIA'S ROOM — NIGHT

14 or 15 year old Mia is asleep in her bed as her
door creeps open... the light from the other room
briefly lights up the room as a man enters.

Seen from behind, the man goes to Mia's window and closes the curtains so that the room
is almost pitch black... the only light coming
in... At the top of the window where the curtains
don't cover.

Hearing the curtains close, Mia wakes up and
looks around. Her eyes not able to focus on the
person in her room but... she inhales deeply.

> MIA (V.O.)
> Same smell.

The man approaches Mia's bed and pulls down the covers as Mia struggles to stay covered up. This tug-o-war continues for a few moments until the man overpowers Mia and rips the covers out of her hands.

                    MIA (V.O.)
     The first time... I will never forget...
     that smell...

Mia lays in her bed... frozen... as the man caresses her legs.

As the man moves his hand up her leg toward her private parts, Mia jerks her body as she is incredibly uncomfortable.

END FLASHBACK

INT. HOSPITAL — ICU — CONTINUOUS

The Head Nurse is now right next to Mia, checking her I.V. Suddenly, Mia's body jerks... startling the hell out of the Head Nurse.

                    MIA (V.O.)
     Where did you get that smell, Nurse?

The Head Nurse finishes her routine check and exits the room. As she exits, Brooke Hill enters and goes to Mia's side.

Brooke sits in silence... looking down somberly at Mia. Something is on Brooke's mind.

The longer Brooke stares at Mia, the more upset she gets. Brooke shakes her head incessantly as a tear runs down her face.

> BROOKE
> (Quietly)
>
> I'm sorry, Mia. I should have said something.

> MIA (V.O.)
> (Incredulously) You knew?

> BROOKE
> But I didn't want to believe it.

BEGIN FLASHBACK

EXT. APARTMENT COMPLEX COURTYARD — NIGHT

A wide view of the courtyard frames many of the apartments in the complex.

In complete darkness, Brooke is looking out the window of one of the apartments. To be more accurate... she is doing her part as a participant in the neighborhood watch program.

> BROOKE (V.O.)
> Because I knew... once I said something... my life would never be the same.

Brooke sees the Daniels' apartment door open.

> BROOKE (V.O.)
> How selfish of me. (Cynically)
>
> My life?

> MIA (V.O.)
> (Angrily) Your life?!

> BROOKE (V.O.)
> What about your life?

Brooke's expression turns to shock and disbelief as HER HUSBAND, Steve Hill, is the person coming out of the Daniels' apartment.

> BROOKE (V.O.)
> I tried to pretend it was Linda but... I knew she wasn't home.

As Steve walks toward their apartment, Brooke rushes away from the window so that Steve doesn't see her.

END FLASHBACK

INT. HOSPITAL — ICU — CONTINUOUS

Brooke stands looking at Mia... now with a face full of tears streaming down her face.

> BROOKE
> Why didn't you say something? (Beat)
> Tell somebody...

> MIA (V.O.)
> Why didn't you DO something? (Scoffs)
> And would you believe a girl who got pregnant at 15?
> (Sadly) Nobody.

> BROOKE
> I was weak and afraid. And you... I wish I was as strong as you were... to have to live with that.

LINDA (O.S)
(Suspiciously) To live with what?

Brooke is startled as she turns to see Linda standing at the door... wearing an unpleasant expression.

BROOKE
Whatever made her feel like she had to do this.

Linda is in a very different state of mind than usual. She appears to be extremely aggressive... her breathing is faster than normal... and her pupils are dilated.

LINDA
What are you trying to say, Brooke?

Brooke sees that Linda is looking for a fight so she does her best to try to calm Linda down.

BROOKE
I'm not trying to say anything, Linda.
(Beat)
I'm just saying that I know what a great girl Mia is.
(Sincerely)
Just trying to understand why.

Linda approaches Brooke and stands very close to her.

LINDA
Oh... I'm sure you have some idea.

Linda peers at Brooke with rage in her eyes. Brooke knows exactly what Linda means and drops her head in shame.

                    BROOKE
    I'm... sorry.

Brooke drags herself toward the door.

                    LINDA
    You should be.

Brooke doesn't even look back as she exits the room... completely devastated.

Linda watches Brooke leave and then turns her attention to Mia.

                    LINDA (CONT'D)
    And you too!
    (Furiously)
    Did you do this to get attention?

                    MIA (V.O.)
    (Mockingly) And here we go...
    (Beat)
    What drug is causing this irrational behavior?

                    LINDA
    Did you do this to ruin my life?

                    MIA (V.O.)
    You're doing a good job of that yourself.

Linda begins to pace around the room as she continues her onslaught.

                    LINDA
I mean... you've done some selfish things
in your life but this... this is the most
selfish thing you could do.

Linda stops pacing and gets serious.

                 LINDA (CONT'D)
(Sincerely) Do you hate me?

Linda walks over and stares calmly at Mia for
several moments.

                 LINDA (CONT'D)
(Deflated)

I know you hate me.

                  MIA (V.O.)
That's the crazy thing... I loved you. But
you never loved me.

                    LINDA
And you should. (Sorrowfully)

You should.

Linda breaks down and cries... but suddenly, she
gets angry.

                 LINDA (CONT'D)
(Angrily) Why?!

(Irately)

Why would you do this?! (Intensely)

All I wanted was to be happy! (Calmly)

And then you came into my life.

Linda looks lovingly at Mia.

                    LINDA (CONT'D)
     (Endearingly) And I was.

     (Beat)

     So why did you try to kill my happiness?

Linda's expression changes yet again... back
to rage.

                    LINDA (CONT'D)
     I hate you for that!

                    TRACY (O.S.)
     Auntie! Why are you talking to Mia like that?

Linda spins around quickly as she is caught off-
guard by Tracy.

                    TRACY (CONT'D)
     That's not going to help her recover.

                    LINDA
     You're right, Trace. (Beat)

     I need a break. This place is depressing.

Linda exits the room as Tracy turns her attention
to Mia.

                    TRACY
     Cousin... I'm here... just me.

Tracy reaches down to hold Mia's hand and drops
her head.

                    TRACY (CONT'D)
I had to come... alone... so I could tell
you that I'm sorry.

(Beat)

I'm so sorry for saying and doing all those
mean things to you.

Tears begin to roll down Tracy's face.

                    TRACY (CONT'D)
I'm sorry for not being able to stand up to
my sisters for you.

(Laughs)

I did once, you know...

BEGIN FLASHBACK

INT. SCHOOL HALLWAY — DAY

Mia hurries down the hallway as female voices
call to her.

                    STEPHANIE (O.C.)
Excuse me, Sir... can you tell me where you
got your outfit? I wanna get it for my Dad.

The students laugh again.

                    TRACY (O.C.)
Everything but the shoes because... what
are those?!?!

Mia stops and turns around as the students erupt
with laughter again.

                         MIA

Why?

                    TASHA (O.C.)
Wait, y'all! It's Mia. Sorry, Mia. We should
have known it was you... by your smell.

(Beat) Woo!

                         MIA

Are you done?

Mia peers sadly down the hallway at her tor-
menters... the COLLINS SISTERS!

Mia locks eyes with Tracy who is laughing along
with her sisters and everyone else. You can lit-
erally see Mia's heart break in that moment and
she turns and races away.

    Immediately... Tracy stops laughing and
    becomes dispirited as she feels horrible.

Tracy turns to her sisters and shakes her head
at them.

                        TRACY
    This ain't right... she's our cousin.

                      STEPHANIE
(Fiercely)

She ain't my cousin.

Tasha looks at Stephanie who is wearing a scowl
and then weighs in.

    TASHA
    It's either her or us.

Tracy looks in the direction Mia ran off in and sees kids still laughing. Then she looks at her sisters and reluctantly makes her choice.

                    TRACY
    Sisters.

END FLASHBACK

INT. HOSPITAL — ICU — CONTINUOUS

Tracy is now holding Mia's hand in both of her hands... sobbing.

                    TRACY
    I'm sorry for making that choice, Cousin.

                 MIA (V.O.)
    I actually believe you... (Beat)
    You were always different than your sisters.

                    TRACY
    Please forgive me.

                 MIA (V.O.)
    (Sincerely)
    I forgive you... Cousin.

Suddenly, Mia's heart monitor reading changes... her heart beat gets stronger.

Tracy notices the change... which startles her so she kisses Mia on the forehead and then exits the room.

INT. HOSPITAL WAITING ROOM — MOMENTS LATER

The waiting room is much less crowded than it has
been but there are still people there to support... including Tina Parker and Miss Clarita
who gets up when she sees Tracy enter the room.

                    TRACY
  (Smiling) Let's go, Grams.

                MISS CLARITA
  Okay, Bay-bee.Miss Clarita is concerned but
  doesn't want to show it.

              MISS CLARITA (CONT'D)
  (Probing)

  Ya visit was good?

Tracy smiles and nods her head as they walk out
of the waiting room... Miss Clarita wearing a
slight grin.

Shannon is in the waiting room sitting facing the
hospital hallway. Shannon sees Linda about to
enter the room but she goes into the hallway to
meet Linda.

INT. HOSPITAL HALLWAY - CONTINOUS

Shannon notices that Linda seems different.

                   SHANNON
  Mrs. Daniels is Mia okay? You seem upset.

                    LINDA
  No. She's not okay. She's dying... and it's
  my fault.

Shannon remains silent and just listens as
Linda breaks down.

LINDA (CONT'D)
I thought I could handle it. I was in control.

(Scoff)

I could stop whenever I wanted, right?

(Beat)

And when Mia came into my life... I did...
for a while.

SHANNON
I'm sorry, Mrs. Daniels... what did you stop?

LINDA
Drinking...

(Beat)

The first three years Mia was in my life...
I stopped drinking... cold turkey.

Linda laughs to herself.

LINDA (CONT'D)
Because that's what you do, right? Better
yourself for your child?

SHANNON
Yes... and it sounds like you did.

LINDA
(Sarcastic laugh)

Until I lost my job and ended up in a
homeless shelter.

SHANNON
Oh my goodness. What happened?

                    LINDA
(Deadly serious) Drugs.

(Beat)

Hit me harder than alcohol.

Shannon listens sympathetically... nodding her
head... but taking mental notes.

                LINDA (CONT'D)
Made me do so many things that I hate.

(Beat)

Caused me to damage my relationship with Mia.

Linda listens to her own words and shakes her
head in disbelief.

                LINDA (CONT'D)
And even when I tried to fix it... to make
up for what I did... by changing my life.
Trying to give me and Mia some stability...

(Sadly)

The man I brought into our lives... just
made things worse.

A light bulb goes on in Shannon's mind... now
things are starting to come together and Shannon
probes a little more.

                SHANNON
Do you mean, John?

Almost on cue, John enters the waiting room and
spots Linda talking to Shannon and rushes over
to them.

John plants his customary kiss on Linda's lips but stares into her eyes as he slowly pulls away... and notices that her pupils are dilated.

                    JOHN
        (To Linda)

        Hey, Sweetheart... the doctor wants to talk
        to us in Mia's room right now.

John forces a smile at Shannon.

                JOHN (CONT'D)
        Please excuse us, Ms. Price.

Before Shannon can respond, John whisks Linda away and down the hallway.

INT . HOSPITAL - ICU - MOMENT LATER

John forcibly ushers linda into mia's hospital room and look to make sure there are no nurses in the room . once he's certain they are alone ... he closes the door.

Immediately, john's face contorts in such a way that it makes linda uncomfortable.

                    JOHN
        (STERNLY)

        what was that out there?

        (interrogating)

        what the hell were you about to tell
        that reporter?

        linda looks at mia... then back to john.

                    LINDA
keep your voice down.

john is not having this...

                    JOHN
(ferociously)
who you think you're talking to?

                    LINDA
(quietly)
she can hear you.

john looks around incredulously and scoffs

                    JOHN
you still believe anything ... just

like when i first meet you.

(beat)

mia can't hear anything

(condescendingly)

she's lucky to even be alive ...no thanks
to you

This verbal low blow nearly floors linda

                    LINDA
(dejectedly)
why do you have to be such an asshole?

linda looks at john, smirks, and then works out
of the room.

john smiles deviously and crosses to mia's beside. He looks down at her and takes her hand in his.

john bend down and gets close to mia's ear.

                    JOHN
    (softly)
    mia...can you hear me ?
    (MORE)

                JOHN (CONT'D)
    (whispering)
    can you hear me, Baby?

                    MIA (V.O)
    i wish i couldn't.
    (beat)
    Too many lies...
    (skeptically)
    Baby?

BEGIN FLASHBACK

INT. MOTEL ROOM - DAY

john sits up in a bed ... partially dressed ...partially under the covers ... looking toward the bathroom door.

                    JOHN
    Baby! come out; i want to see you.
    (seductively)
    come out, Baby.

seconds later ... MIA WALKS OUT OF THE
BATHROOM...wearing a RED SKIMPY NEFLIGEE. mia is
clearly uncomfortable in this outfit but she mod-
els it for john who is all about it!

> JOHN (CONT'D)
> Damn, Baby! unh. uhnm!

mia blushes.

> MIA9I
> I'M only wearing this for you.

> JOHN
> you better be only wearing that for me.
> mia laughs

> MIA
> you know that i mean, Baby.
> john gives mia a knowing look and smiles
> at her.

> JOHN
> (nodding)
> come here.

mia smiles and gets in the bed. john raps himself
around her and mia melts melts into his embrace.

> MIA
> I could do this forever.

> JOHN
> me too baby.

> MIA (V.O)
> how dumb was i to believe you?

END FLASHBACK

INT. HOSPITAL - ICU - CONTINOUS

john looks out the window of the room and sees
the head nurse. immediately, he sits in the chair
next to mia and lays his head on mia's arm...all
for show.

EXT. HOSPITAL - ICU - CONTINOUS

Shannon walks up behind the head nurse and sees
her fawning over john but the head nurse doesn't
know Shannon is there.

Shannon also observes how john is interacting
with mia... holding her hand ... caressing her
arm...

> SHANNON
> he seems like such a good man, right?
>
> the head nurse spins around quickly ...
> slightly surprised ...slightly embarrassed

> HEAD NURSE
> (smiling to herself)
>
> He's a really good man.

The head nurse snaps out of her daze.

> HEAD NURSE (CONT'D)
> (professionally)
>
> uh...yes ...he really cares about his step
> step- daughter

                    SHANNON
    it's a little stranger that he's here here
    and her mother isn't.

The head nurse sheds a slight smiles.

                    HEAD NURSE
    well...they has a little disagreement
    earlier and the wife left.

                    SHANNON
    Do you know the disagreement was about you?

                    HEAD NURSE
    I wasn't really listening but...something
    about who was responsible for this.

Shannon peers at the head nurse curiously.

INT. HOSPITAL - ICU - CONTINOUS

John stands up and looks down at mia.

                    JOHN
    if you can hear me ...
    (smirks)
    i hope you can hear me..
    (endearingly)
    you know what would be so amazing?

john gets close to mia's ear and whispers something inaudible to everyone except mia.

suddenly, mia's monitor begin to "freak out."

john scoffs and moves away from mia...shaking his
head as the team of nurses rush in.

john exits the room ... surprised to see Shannon.

JOHN (CONT'D)
you certainly are going above and beyond,
ms. price.

SHANNON
That's the only way truth comes out.

JOHN
Not all people want their truth out there.

(beat)

i think you, of all people, would agree,
right, Ms. price.

john wearing a smug grin. Shannon sheds an
equally loaded grin.

SHANNON
Based on what I've seen ...i think you might
be able to answer that better than me.

(beat)

I know who you are.

John reverts to his super practiced smiles.

JOHN
Be careful, Ms . price. most people with
secrets ... want them to say buried.

(threateningly)

Diddy too deep ... you're bound to end up
with the skeletons.

john laughs sarcastically ... pleased with himself... he strolls away confidently as Shannon
watches ...quietly fuming.

EXT. HOSPITAL - ICU - CONTINOUS

As john exits the room he takes out his cellphone
and makes a call.

                    JOHN
     (into the phone)
     we have a situation ...

EXT. HOSPITAL PARKING LOT - MOMENTS LATER

Shannon walks into the parking lot and is amazed
at the crowd. it is much larger than it has been
... filled with supporters not just from within
Mia's immediate community... but from all over
the city.

Shannon spots david and goes to him.

                    SHANNON
     why are all these people here tonight?

David appears a bit on edge.

                    DAVID
     Alot of them said them said they saw our
     coverage and wanted to do something to help.

                    SHANNON
     That's amazing! means we're doing our job.

David expression indicates that he doesn't agree.

                    DAVID
     (shaking his head)
     what we're doing is shining a spotlight on
     this community ...

which might not be a good thing.

Shannon peers at david curiously ...

>   SHANNON
> Making people aware is always good...

>   DAVID
> In a perfect world ... maybe. but

this community ain't even close.

Shannon glares at david. ''what is your problem?" she thinks and it comes out in her slightly irritated response.

>   SHANNON
> You sound like you don't want anything good
> in your hood

Shannon looks around.

>   SHANNON (CONT'D)
> Hopefully most of this people are here
> because they do.

Shannon turns away from david and stops the first person she sees... a 20- something white guy who's exquisitely put together outfit and over- done head movements scream, "i'm liberal ...and gay!"

>   SHANNON (CONT'D)
> Excuse me, sir.

The liberal guy spins around flamboyantly.

>   LIBERAL GUY
> Yes, honey?

Shannon motions for david to gets his camera ready.

> SHANNON
>
> What brought you out tonight?

> LIBERAL GUY
>
> Well, YOU... in all your fabulousness!

Shannon laughs.

> SHANNON
>
> Well... thank you. But ...i'm sure you're aware that there is a much bigger cause we're supporting here.

> LIBERAL GUY
>
> Of course ... and it just breaks my heart because this could have been avoided.
>
> (beats)
>
> if we have stickers gun laws.

> SHANNON
>
> So you think this tragedy is the result is the results of our guns laws?

> LIBERAL GUY
>
> Every person who can buy a gun, doesn't necessarily need to have one.
>
> (beat)
>
> less guns on the streets. less shooting.

David shouts angrily from behind the camera.

> DAVID
>
> This wasn't a shooting. Genius!

Shannon gives david the "cut" sign and he lowers
the camera as the liberal guy saunters away.

                    SHANNON
    What's going on with you tonight?

    you've been on edge since i got here.

                    DAVID
    (with slight attitude)

    i'm good. let's just keep going.

Shannon turns searches for someone else to
interview and finds...JACKIE KEENE... a larger
white woman who's eyes are true blue and filled
with sadness

                    SHANNON
    Hello ma'am. i'm Shannon price,

    news 9. can i ask you why you are here
    tonight ?

                    JACKIE
    (holding back tears)

    i don't know... really.

                    SHANON
    Do you know why this crowd is gathered?

                    JACKIE
    (nodding her head)

    it's all too familiar.

    (tearing up)

    After all this years ... you'd think ... it
    would'nt still hurt so much.

                    SHANNON
    what wouldn't

                         JACKIE
My 16 years old sister committed suicide
10 years ago and it feels like it happened
just yesterday.

This hits Shannon hard and her expression immediately become mournful.

                        SHANNON
I'm so sorry for your loss.

(beat)

can you share anything from your experience
that might help others?

jackie pulls herself together and stops crying
....she looks directly into the camera with pro-
nounced seriousness.

                         JACKIE
Suicide is NOT the answer . it's the easy way
out... for the person that does it but...hell for
those they leave behind.

                        SHANNON
A permanent choice for a temporary situation

jackie nods her head in agreement.

                   SHANNON (CONT'D)
Thank you for sharing your story. i know
it's going to help someone out there.

jackie smile and gives Shannon a tight hug
...catching Shannon off guard

As Shannon looks over jackie's shoulder, she spots on a group of people standing in a cir-cle....seemingly praying.

Shannon gently pulls away from jackie, smiles at her, and then heads toward the circle as david follows.

As shannnon and david approached the group, they see that each member of the group is holding a picture boy.

SHANNON (CONT'D)
Excuse me. may i ask who the young boy in the photo is?

A conservatively dressed, very fit, early 30's MAN and a late 20's WOMAN dressed in equally conser-vative business attire break the circle and move toward Shannon.

MAN
I'm mare and this is my wife, caroline

(holding up the photo)

This is our son, joaquin. he was 10 years when he takes his life.

Marc's voice cracks at the end of his sentence and caroline jumps in.

CAROLINE
He was a victim of bulling. cyber and physical.

Shannon is emotionally impacted as her eyes will up with tears.

SHANNON
(choking back tears)

oh my goodness. i am so sorry. i can't even imagine.

MARC
Neither could we. joaquin was an amazing boy with a heart of gold.

CAROLINE
We didn't see any signs until it was too late.

SHANNON
Do you mind sharing your story?

CAROLINE
Apparently, some kids would tease joaquin because he was small for his age.

MARC.
So i was ... at his age

CAROLINE
And because he was such a nice boy who wasn't doing what others the other boys his age were doing ... like playing baseball.... they taunted and accused him of being gay.

MARC
What do kids that age even know about that stuff? who are they learning it from?

SHANNON
When did you learn of the bulling?

CAROLINE
After he dead.

caroline gets very somber and stops talking.

                    MARC

Evidently, it was happening for quite a
while and joaquin told his teachers but hey
never told us about it ... just attributing
it to "kids being kids".

(beat)

i just don't understand why he didn't say
anything to us.

caroline grabs the mic and looks directly
into camera.

                   CAROLINE

Words. hurts. spoken words AND written
words. words you think are funny. words you
think aren't bad.

(tearing up)

You don't know how heartfelt your words can
be or... the pain they can cause.

caroline breaks down sobbing and marc com-
forts her.

                   SHANNON

Thank you for sharing your heartbroken
story. I know it can't bring joaquin back
but hopefully, you sharing your experience
will shine a light on the seriousness of
bullying and the hurt it causes.

(beat)

This is Shannon price, News 9.

As Shannon gives david the "cut" sign, she sees
PK standing in close proximity looking like she
want to talk.

SHANNON (CONT'D)

(to david)

stay here i'll be back.

Shannon goes to PK.

SHANNON (CONT'D)

Hey PK. you okay?

PK

i need to tell you something.

SHANNON

Ok i'm listening.

PK

I had a strange conversation with mia a few weeks ago. she was sad...almost depressed.

(beat)

But... she kept talking about her stepfather and how he was the only person who really understood her.

Shannon is listening intently.

PK (CONT'D)

I didn't think anything of it then but now... it was weird...

(hesitantly)

it was almost like she was in love with him.

BINGO! And now Shannon understands what's going on.

SHANNON

Thank you for sharing. PK. You're a good friend. keep this to yourself for now

...i'm going to get to the bottom of this
...for mia.

PK smiles at Shannon who smiles back.

INT. HOSPITAL - ICU - NIGHT

Linda enters the room and smiles as the strides
toward mia's bed. she's clearly in a better place
than she was the last time she was in the space.

linda looks endearingly at mia.

                    LINDA
You'd be happy to know that i went back to
my sponsor.
(beat)
I'm going to get and stay clean.
for me this time ....and for you.

linda takes mia's hand.

                    LINDA (CONT'D)
You were put in my care for a reasons
and....i'm sorry for letting you down.
(beat)
for letting my demons become your demons.
(beat)
You didn't deserve this.

Linda take a HUGE deep breath.

                    LINDA (CONT'D)
I don't know if you can hear me but...for
the first time in a long time ... i have
clarity... and i want to know something.

(beats)

You... are an amazing daughter. so smart...
creative... and strong.

(smirks)

much stronger than me.

mia's heart monitor begin to beep stronger.

                    MIA (V .O)
I haven't seen this person in a very
long time.

                    LINDA
I Played the victim for way too long.

(beat)

You don't know this but... i was abused
as child...my father physically abused my
mother and me....sexually.

Linda starts to cry.

                    LINDA (CONT'D)
That really messes a person up.

(beat)

I let it define me...and acted accordingly
because...

(MORE)

> LINDA (CONT'D)

I was the victim.

(beat)

it caused me to stay silent when i shouldn't have.

BEGIN FLASHBACK - Repay of earlier flashback but from linda's POV.

INT. APARTMENT - NIGHT

Mia is in their apartment being yelled at by john while linda watches from the couch silently... staring blankly...appearing almost confused by what's happening.

In fronts of linda on the table is an open bottle of Oxycontin.

from linda's POV, the scene is moving in slow motion.

> JOHN

(to mia)

yo

You coming into my house accusing and disrespecting me?

(angrily)

You must have lost your mind, little girl.

(dismissively)

You need to get the hell of my house with all that bullshit.

Mia looks to linda ....trying to connect with her mother so she can step in but.... linda remain dazed and confused on the couch.

Mia sees this, and runs out of the apartment.

Once linda sees this... the scene returns to normal motion and linda sees this... the scene returns to normal motion and linda stands up and rushes to the door but john stops her.

> JOHN (CONT'D)
> (irritated)
>
> where you going? sit your high ass down and take another one of those pills i gave you.
>
> (scoffs)
>
> linda stands frozen...looking out the door sadly...trying to see where mia ran off to

END FLASHBACK

INT. HOSPITAL - CCU - CONTINOUS

Linda wipes the tears from her eyes.

> LINDA
>
> Because obviously...this was the way things were supposed to be, right?

> MIA (V. O)
>
> you had a choice.

> LINDA
>
> But i was wrong... there's always a different path ....and sometimes....
>
> we have to make our own.

linda breathes deeply again and smiles at mia through hr tears.

> LINDA (CONT'D)
> And you were, Me..Me...you were.
> (beat)
> And i am so proud of you.
> (sobbing)
> You have to wake up. i need... you.

Linda bends down and puts her mouth close to mia's ear.

> LINDA (CONT'D)
> You really are the best thing that has ever happened to me.

Linda kisses mia on the forehead and turns to leave the room.

> MIA (V. O.)
> Do you know how many times i wish you really meant that?

Mia's heart monitor begins to keep stronger.

EXT. HOMELESS SHELTER - DAY

Shannon and david approach the entrance of homeless shelter.Shannon is on a mission as david tracks behind her slowly.

Shannon stops at the door to give david instructions..

                    SHANNON
    Start rolling as soon as i start talking to
    john daniels.

David nods hesitantly as Shannon opens the door
and walks in.

INT. HOMELESS - CONTINOUS

Shannon approaches the first person she sees
...a JANITOR

                    SHANNON
    Excuse me.... im looking for john

    Daniels. Have you seen him?

The janitor nervously shakes his head and hurries away.

Shannon questions a few other people....with the
same result ... no one has seen john.

After a few moments ....Mr Berg strolls out of
his office toward shannon and david. Shannon gives
david the signal to begin filming.

                    MR BERG
    You can't come into my establishment and
    start harassing my staff, Ms.price

Mr Berg notices that david is fliming and gives
david a look and subtly shakes his head and...
David stops filming and lowers his camera.

                    SHANNON
    I'm not harassing anyone, Mr. Berg...just
    looking for john daniels.

(beat)

it's your staff that's acting like they have something to hide.

                    MR. BERG
The fact finder in you should already know that john works at night.

                    SHANNON
Well, a pretty reliable source told me that he came in today.

                    MR. BERG
You can't believe everything you hear, Ms. price. you have to be able to prove it.

(smirks)

No evidence...no case.

Mr. Berg flashes an arrogant smile irritate Shannon but she doesn't respond

                MR BERG (CONT'D)
And as far as my staff's behavior... we are all still grieving the death of one of our occupants.

Shannon's eyes perk up.

                MR BERG(CONT'D)
Even though we don't know a lot about the people who stay here... a loss is always sad.

(beat)

I just knew her a Debra.

Shannon peers intensely into Mr. Berg's eyes....
she is angry and sad at the same time.

                    SHANNON
How did she die?

                    MR. BERG
We don't know yet. autopsy results aren't
back... she appeared to be a user. so most
likely ...an overdose.

(insincerely)

still sad though.....

                    SHANNON
Did she gets the drugs here?

                    MR. BERG
I can assure you, she did not get them here.
my facilities are clean.... no drugs or
alcohol allowed.

Shannon glares skeptically at Mr. Berg who
returns the scowl.

suddenly, Mr. Berg's apple watch beeps....inter-
rupting the stare down. he looks at his wrist.

              MR. BERG (CONT'D)
Any other questions, Ms. prince. i have to
get to a meeting.

                    SHANNON
No, i don't. But next time, i'll make sure
to have evidence.

Mr. Berg flashes an insincere smile.

                    MR BERG
oh... and one other thing i remember about
Debra...

(devious smile)

she loved the chicken soup here.

Shannon eyes get big as she recalls her initial conversation with debra.

BEGIN FLASHBACK

EXT. HOMELESS SHELTER - DAY

Shannon looks skeptically at debra.

> DEBRA
> (sarcastic chuckle)
> You think i come here for the chicken noodle soup?

Debra pulls up her sleeves and holds out her arms ....revealing several track marks.

BEGIN FLASHBACK

INT. HOMELESS SHELTER - CONTINOUS

Mr. Berg struts away.... sarcastically chuck- ing to himself as Shannon stares daggers in his direction.

> SHANNON
> (to david)
> He's lying. And i know he did something to that woman.

> DAVID
> Maybe that woman did something to him. i told you before ... leave Berg alone.
> (beat)

A man like that has secrets he doesn't
want exposed.

Shannon stares curiously at david but
remains silent.

>   DAVID (CONT'D)
>   There's already been one death here ...let's
>   keep it that way.

Shannon shakes her head in disagreement.

>   SHANNON
>   I couldn't put my finger on it before now ...
>   i get it. before but now ...i get it.
>   (beat)

David is stunned.He doesn't respond but the look
on his face speaks volumes.

BEGIN FLASHBACK

INT. MIA'S ROOM - NIGHT

mia is sitting up in her bed ...with an unfa-
miliar look of determination. something in her
is different.

mia's bedroom door opens and....david creeps in.
He looks at Mia an unbuttons his shirts.

Mia's pulls the blanket up to her chin as she
watches david undressed.

David walks over to Mia and tries to pull the
blanket down but... Mia resists. he tries
again..... and again ...Mia resists.

> DAVID

What's wrong?

> MIA

No more

> DAVID

What? i thought you liked me.

David tries to pull down the blanket again. Mia doesn't let him and they begin to struggle.

David gets angry as mia is holding her own.... keeping off of her

> David (contd)

Come on you little slut

This infuriates mia and she kicks david in the balls ! David yells and crumples to the ground.

> Mia

I am not a slut, you pervert

David is still in pain but crawls around on the floor collecting his clothes and makes his way to the door.

Mia hops out of bed feeling triumphant and opens the door.

As david exits ......Mia slams the door behind him.... wearing a huge smile.

End FLASHBACK

INT HOMELESS SHELTER DAY

shannon is still staring at david ...... waiting
for him to response.

                    David
    Its complicated Shannon.......and i
    cannot risk not being around for my girl.

                    Shannon
    the truth always comes out D

    I am going to figure this out.

David looks pensive but doesn't respond

Shannon turns towards the door and as she goes to
exits the shelter....... She stops dead in her
tracks.

Shannon walks slowly towards a wall of framed
photos and focuses on one photo .... a man and a
woman posing with Mr. and Mrs. Breg at the grand
opening of the shelter

Shannon takes out her phone and snaps a picture
of the photo and then rushes out...

Once Shannon is gone... Mr Berg and John approach
David from behind.

                    MR BERG
    Your   reporter   friend   has   become   a
    real problem.

    (beat)

    And we can't have any problems.

David don,t move or respond... he just stands there... dispirited.

EXT. PRICE FAMILY HOME - DAY

Shannon appears hesitant as she walks along a pave stone pathway which splits the perfectly manicured lawn of a large and luxurious model-es-que home.

As Shannon gets to the door, she takes a deep breath and rings the doorbell.

The door opens and standing there is very well put together woman. CELESTE PRICE. Her perfect hair, perfect makeup, and trendy outfit might fool you into thinking she is Shannon's slightly older sister but...

                    SHANNON
     Sorry i didn't call first, Mom, but this
     is important.

Celeste flashes a courtesy smile

                    CELESTE
     Hello to you too, Daughter, come in.

INT. PRICE FAMILY HOME - MOMENTS LATER

Shannon and her mother sit across from each other in gaudy oversized chairs. Celeste is relaxed. Shannon appears nervous.

                    CELESTE
     Can i get you something to calm your serves?

SHANNON

No, thank you. i won't stay long.

CELESTE (CONT'D)

Shannon goes into her purse and pulls out her cellphone. she opens her phone to the photo she snapped at the shelter...the one with the man and woman with Mr.Berg at the grand opening of the shelter...and shows celeste.

Celeste smiles and chuckles to herself.

CELESTE (CONT'D)

Who are those young people ?

SHANNON

(slightly irritated)

You and dad.

CELESTE

Watch your tone, young lady.

(beat)

what's the problem ?

SHANNON

The problem is.....you and dad are all buddy... buddy with a knows drug kingpin.

Celeste frowns.

CELESTE

Despite what you think you know about Alexander Berg, back when we took that picture , he was just a man who did something good for his community.

SHANNON

Well, he's not doing good now.

                    CELESTE

I understand you blame him for getting you
fired from your big time news job but ... you
brought that on yourself.

(beat)

You over stepped and invaded his privacy
.... without cause.

Shannon listens without responding.clearly this
is difficult for her to hear.

                 CELESTE (CONT'D)

So, the only person you should be mad at....
is you.

(jabbing)

You should have use this persistence for
medical school like we planned and you could
have avoided that embarrassment.

(sarcastically)

And so we could.

                    SHANNON

Clearly, this was a bad idea.

Shannon gathers her things and gets up
to leave.

                    CELESTE

What did you expect? you come here after
all these years and question me about my
old friends.

(MORE)

                 CELESTE (CONT'D)

One of whom helped you out with your
big problem.

Shannon drops her hand ...she knows exactly what her mother is talking about.

> CELESTE (CONT'D)
> Lynn Berg was the social worker on your case. i couldn't do it because you are my daughter. but lynn and i worked together for years so i knew i could trust her to take care of you and your baby.

Immediately, Shannon flashes back to a time when she was 16 and PREGNAT.

INT.HOSPITAL DELIVERY ROOM - DAY

16 year old Shannon lays uncomfortably in a hospital bed as a younger and not as flawless Celeste and LYNN BERG,

also younger and frumpy, monitor her condition.

> CELESTE
> Lynn is here from social service and she will take the baby once it is born.

> SHANNON
> She... when she is born.

> LYNN
> When she is born, we are going to take her to a nice family that can't wait to adopt her.

Shannon looks sad.

> SHANNON
> Can't hold her... just once?

                    CELESTE
        It's best not to get attracted.

Lynn smiles at Shannon.

                     LYNN
        One time won't hurt.

Shannon smiles at lynn.

INT. HOSPITAL DELIVERY ROOM - LATER

Shannon is asleep in bed... she's alone in her
room but in her head she hears a baby crying she
opens her eyes and tries to sit up but she can't
...she is in a lot of pain.

                   CELESTE
        You did good, baby.

Shannon looks around...almost panicked.

                   SHANNON
        Where is she? where is my baby?

                   CELESTE
        Sweetheart...she's not yours.

Shannon is crushed and begins crying.

                   SHANNON
        You said i could hold her.

lynn walks in holding the baby and goes
to Shannon.

                    LYNN
     And you can't...here she is.

lynn puts the baby on shannon's chest and Shannon
immediately falls in love.

Shannon gets to hold the baby girl for a few
moments then lynn comes over and tries to take
her. but Shannon refuses.

                    SHANNON
     just a few more minutes.

                    LYNN
     It's time to let go.

Shannon doesn't let go. she holds on tighter.

                    CELESTE
     (sternly)
     Shannon Lashawn price! lets go!

Shannon lets go... kinda... and as lynn takes the
baby... the swaddle comes undone and last thing
Shannon sees is that the baby has a HERT -SHAPED
BIRTHMARK on her chest.

END FLASHBACK

INT. PRICE FAMILY HOME - CONTINOUS

Shannon stands sadly in front of celeste.

                    SHANNON
     I will regret that decision for the rest of
     my life.

Shannon turns away and slinks toward the
door... dejectedly.

Celeste actually appears to be sad too as she
watches Shannon leave.

INT SHANNON'S CAR -MOMENTS LATER

Still in a sad daze, Shannon hears a baby crying
in her head as she drives off.

As she gets a ways down the road, a car gets on
her tail. she doesn't notice as she is still
reflecting on her painful memory.

Suddenly the car gets on the side of shannon's
car and honks .... startling her. Shannon tries
to stay away from the car but the car keep moving
closer to her car.

In an attempt not to collide with the other
car, Shannon swerves off the road and goes into
a ditch.

The other car stops ... and shannon's cellphone
rings. she answer it.

                    VOICE
     That was just a warning.

The call drops and the car speeds off. shannon's
scrambles to get a picture of the licence plate
but she can't.

Shannon begins to pick up the contents of her
purse that spilled as she drove into the ditch

notices the cellphone that she found near the daniels' apartment.

she tries to turn it on but it's an iPhone and she has an iPhone charger. so she plugs it in, puts it on her seat, and drives off.

EXT. HOSPITAL PARKING LOT - DAY

People are still gathered to support Mia and the community. Shannon is in the middle of the crowd with a determined look on her face. David seems downcast as he films Shannon.

                SHANNON
   To all those watching and listening to thus
   broadcast .... the Mia unfortunate set of
   events occurring in our community.

As Shannon speaks, people all over the community watch her the broadcast.

INT. SMALL HOUSE - CONTINOUS

Miss clarita sits in a chair sadly watching the coverage.

                SHANNON (O.S)
   And what's sad is....if we all came together,
   we could make a difference. we could improve
   the lives of so many others.

INT. APARTMENT -LIVING ROOM - CONTINOUS

Tina parker is sitting on her couch... her two girls laying on her lap. she looks down lovingly at them and gently caresses their heads.

                    SHANNON (O. S)
If we stop letting things slide and just...
speak up.

EXT. HOSPITAL PARKING LOT - CONTINOUS

Pastor Kramer approaches Shannon.

                  PASTOR KRAMER
Exactly, Ms. prince. the good book says in
James, chapter 4 verse 17, 'Therefore, to
him who knows to do good and does not do it,
to him it is sin".

INT. APARTMENT - ROOM - CONTINOUS

Brooke hill lays in her bed with a mournful look
on her face.... she appears to be contemplating
something as she stares at her husband, sterve,
and shake her head sadly. steve smiles at brooke
as pastor kramer continues his mini sermon but
brooke remains stoic.

    (beat)

                  PASTOR KRAMER (O.S.)
We, as a community, have to speak up
and do what's right. Because that's what
God commands.

    (beat)

And obedience to God is most important...
no matter what.

INT HOSPITAL -ICU - CONTINUOUS

Linda is alone in the room with Mia... sitting in the chair next to her... listening to

the machines breath for Mia while gently rubbing her hand.

Linda glances up the television.

> PASTOR KRAMER (O.S.)
> No matter how scary... no matter how uncomfortable... regardless if you've let it go in the past.
> (beat)
> We've got to be better... for each other.

INT. BAR _ CONTINUOUS

The nameless man from Mia's neighborhood who tried to connect with her when he visited her bedroom sits alone at the bar watching the coverage.

> PASTOR KRAMER (O.S.)
> Obviously, we failed young Mia. But let's not repeat our sins and let these kind of tragic events happen again.

Looking into his face... this man is obviously full of anguish. As he continues to listen... one tear... then two... then... a stream flows from his eyes.

The man stands up, pushes his drink away, and drags himself toward the exit.

EXT. HOSPITAL PARKING LOT _ CONTINUOUS

Back in the mix... Shannon is hanging onto every one of Pastor Kramer's words... as is the entire crowd. Pastor Kramer bows his head and closes his eyes

> PASTOR KRAMER
>
> Dear Heavenly Father... thank you for what you are doing and will do in this time. We praise you in advance for the miracle of healing. And not just Mia but... our whole community. We are all broken and in need of your love, your mercy, and in your amazing grace. Please help us to be better... for each other... for you. In Your name we pray... Amen.

"Amen" echoes throughout the crowd.

> PASTOR KRAMER (CONT'D)
> (to Shannon)
>
> I'm sorry, Ms. Price, for turning your broadcast into my pupit.

Shannon wears a satisfied smile.

> SHANNON
>
> No worries, Pastor. People need to hear the truth. So... thank you for that.
> (to the camera)
>
> And thank you to all those who are going to be better. I know i am.
> (beat)
>
> This is Shannon Price reporting live from Huntington Memorial Hospital.

EXT. POLICE STATION - EVENING

Mia's nameless male neighbor stands outside of
the police station at the bottom of the steps...
just staring at the doors.

With a deep sigh and nodding of his head... he
slowly walks up the steps and toward the door.

As the man gets to the top of the steps, Brooke
Hill walks out of the police station... tears in
her eyes.

As they pass each other, Brooke peers at the man
curiously... like she's seen him before.

The man drops his head and enters the
police department.

INT. POLICE STATION - CONTIONOUS

The man scans the station and walks directly to
an officer. He says something to the officer and
the officers takes out his handcuffs and puts them
on the man

EXT. APARTMENT COMPLEX COUNTYARD - DAY

Shannon hustles along the red brick courtyard
toward Linda's apartment but she stops short as
she see   POLICE OFFICERS

leading steve   Hill out in   HANDCUFFS...
steve's head down in shame while Brooke looks
on... tears rolling down her face.

Shannon spots Linda watching the scene from
her doorway

EXT. APARTMENT - CONTINUOUS

Shannon reaches Linda's door as Linda peers
inquisitively at her.

                    SHANNON
    Do you know what that is about?

                    LINDA
    Just another part of the tragedy

                    SHANNON
    How so?

                    LINDA
    Sick men preying on innocent girls.

Shannon picks up on the unspoken truth.

                    SHNNON
    (sadly intuitive)
    Mia?

                LINDA (CONT'D)
    How messed up am I to have let this happen?
    What is wrong with me?

                    SHANNON
    I'm not so sure it was all you.

Linda looks peculiarly at Shannon who digs in her
purse and pulls out a cellphone

                    LINDA
    Where you get that? it's Mia's

                    SHANNON
    I found it in the courtyard.

Linda looks puzzled. Shannon presses'

                    SHNNON (CONT'D)
    Do you know who ''Mr Perfect'' is?

Linda perks up and becomes extremely pensive.

                    SHANNON (CONT'D)
    Well,Mr. perfect wrote this to Mia

    the night she shot herself.

    (reading)

    ''We need to talk. Tonight. Don't worry
    about your mother ... You know I got
    something for her. ''

                    SHANNON (CONT'D)
    Mia wrote back, ''Why are you acting like
    this? you told me you love me and that we
    are going to be together. I told you this
    because you are the only person I trust. ''

Linda listens incredulously but remains silent.

                    SHANNON (CONT'D)
    Look at his reply.

Linda takes the phone and reads.

                    LINDA
    ''You believe anything. Just like your
    mother. You really thought that I loved
    you?''

Linda can't believe her ears but continues to read.

                    LINDA (CONT'D)
Son of a bitch!

                    SHANNON
You know who it is?

                    LINDA
Mia watched wresting because of John. She always used to talk about how she loved Mr Perfect. As a joke i called John that... because I thought he was perfect.

(sadly)

Damn it... he took advantage of me... and her.

(dispirited)

I... can't...

Linda is almost despondent.

                    SHANNON
Justice will be served, Linda.

Linda nods in agreement even though she is not really all there.

EXT. HOSPITAL STAFF SLEEP ROOM - EVENING

The door opens and out walks the Head Nurse... adjusting

her scrubs and her disheveled hair.

She looks around scanning her surroundings. When she sees that on one is looking.. She motions with her hand and races away.

Second later... John quickly exits the room... definitely not inhits

wanting anyone to know he was in there with her.

John sprays a couple of squirts of cologne to mask the sex smell and stroll down the hall-way calmly.

INT. HOSPITAL - ICU - MOMENTS LATER

John enters Mia's room and watches as a nurse conducts an exam on Mia.

                    JOHN
     (falsely hopeful)
     is she improving at all?

The Nurse frowns sorrowfully at john

                    NURSE
     Sometimes she seems so strong.... and
     then...she goes backward.
     (MORE)
                    NURSE (CONT'D)
     (beat)
     I know I'm not supposed to get attached to
     patients but...   I want
     Mia to survive.

John moves closer to Nurse...very close.

                              JOHN
    it just shows that you have compassion.

    (semi-seductively)

    Which is a good quality for someone who
    should have a good bedside manner.

As John finishes his sentence, he pushes up
against the Nurse from behind and the Nurse does
not like it.

She shoots John a look of disgust and exits
the room.

                         MIA (V.O)
    (inhaling)

    That smell is back. I know that smell.

John looks down sweetly at Mia. He takes her
hand. He rubs he head. Then he looks over his
shoulder toward the sliding glass door to see if
anyone is watching him.

When John realizes that he doesn't have an audience, he leans in toward Mia's ear. This time we
can hear what he says to her.

                              JOHN
    I Just don't understand... why?

    (smirks)

    Why are you fighting?

Immediately... Mia goes back to a previous
memory...

BEGIN FLASHBACK

INT. MIA'S ROOM - NIGHT

14 or 15 year old Mia is asleep in her bed as her
door creeps open... the light from the other room
briefly lights up the room as a man enters.

Seen from behind, the man goes to Mia's window and closes the curtains so that the room is
almost pitch black... the only light coming in...
at the room of the window where the curtains
don't cover.

Hearing the curtains close, Mia wake up and looks
around. Her eyes not able to focus on the person
in her room but... she inhales deeply.

The man approaches Mia's bed and pulls down the
covers as Mia struggles to stay covered up.

                    MIA
    No! stop! please!

                    MAN
    Why are you fighting?

This tug-o-war continues for a few moments until
the man overpowers Mia and rips the covers out of
her hands.

    Mia lays in her bed... frozen... as the
    caresses her legs.

As the man moves his hand up her leg toward her
private parts, his face comes into focus. IT
IS JOHN.

END FLASHBACK

INT. HOSPITAL - ICU - CONTINUOUS

                    MIA (V.O)
your cheap cologne... I will never forget
that smell.

(beat)

How many victims have had to smell that
awful smell?

                    JOHN
Are you fighting because you love me?

(charming)

If you love me... make my life easier...

(coldly)

Just die already)

  (heartless)

1. Don't. Love. You.

                    LINDA (O.C)
(irately)

You son of a bitch!

John is caught completely off-guard. He turns
around hesitantly even thought he doesn't want to
and sees Lind standing in the doorway... fuming!

                    LINDA (CONT'D)
How long...Mr perfect?

                    MIA (V.O)
The truth is out now, john. Can't sweet
talk your way out of this one, Mr. perfect.

                    LINDA
How long have you been sleeping with me and
my daughter?

                         JOHN
Your daughter? you're calling her that now?
Because when we met, she was your ticket to
get high.

(beat)

You allowed all those men into her room.
And now you want to come at me crazy?

                         LINDA
You are disgusting. she was just a
little girl.

                         JOHN
Your little approached me...

Daddy issue... like mother, like daughter...

  (smirks)

                         LINDA
So... she was telling the truth that night
you kicked her out.

BEGIN FLASHBACK

INT. APARTMENT - NIGHT

Mia is standing in front of her bedroom door...
crying as she addresses John who glares at
her angrily.

                         MIA
Why are you doing this? you're denying everything? You told me you love me.

John wears a indignant smirk and shakes his
head. Linda watches from the couch silently...
staring blankly... appearing almost confused by
what's happening.

                    MIA (CONT')
You made love to me...

(sadly)

You told me you were going to leave her.

In front of Linda on the table is an open bottle
of Oxycontin... which explains why she appears
''out of it.''

                    JOHN
(to Mia)

What the hell you talking about? You coming
into my house accusing and disrespecting me?

(angrily)

You must have lost yo damn mind, little girl.

(dismissively)

You need to get the hell outta my house with
all that bullshit.

                    MIA
(to Linda)

i'm telling the truth.

Mia looks to Linda... trying to concern with her
mother so she can step in buy...Linda remains
dazed and confused on the couch.

Mia sees this, turns and runs out of
the apartment.

Linda stands up and rushes to the door but john
stops her.

> JOHN

(irritated)

Where you going? Sit your high ass down and take another one of those pills i gave you.

(scoffs)

Do you even know where you are right now?

Linda stands frozen... looking out the door sadly... trying to see where Mia ran off to.

INT. THE PARKER APARTMENT -MOMENTS LATER

Mia sits nervously on the couch in the living room as Tina enters from the halfway.

> TINA

Now that the kids are asleep... I

can actually listen to you.

(MORE)

> TINA (CONT'D)

What's wrong, Mia? what's on your mind? you can tell me, sweetheart.

Mia looks like she wants to say so say something but..... she just breaks down.... sobbing.

> TINA (CONT'D)

Whatever it is.... it's going to be okay..... i promise.

> MIA

I need your help, Mrs. parker.

> TINA

Whatever you need, sweetheart.

kelvins opens the front door, walks in and stares peculiarly at the old scene.

                    KELVIN
     Is everything okay?

Mia hops up suddenly, puts on a brave face, and....

                     MIA
     Thank you, Mrs. parker. i gotta go.

                    TINA
     It's okay, Mia.... you can stay if u need to.

Mia turns and quickly runs out. Tina peers suspiciously at kelvin.

EXT. APARTMENT COMPLEX COURTYARD - CONTINOUS

Mia is making a call on her cellphone.

                     MIA
     PK.... I really need to talk to you. i don't
     have anyone else to talk to, please call
     me back.

EXT. SMALL HOUSE - LATER

     Mia walks slowly along the sidewalk when
     she spots miss clarita's house and walks
     up to the door and knocks. no answer ....
     she knocks again.... still no answer so she
     turns and walks away.

As Mia walks away sadly.... miss clarita
watches from a window

EXT. NEIGHBORHOOD STREET -LATER

Mia is completely alone as she aimlessly wanders
the streets. something catches her eye and she
heads that way.

EXT. HOMELESS SHELTER - MOMENTS LATER

Mia unhappily walks into the shelter as she has
nowhere else to go.

INT. HOMELESS SHELTER - MOMENTS LATER

As Mia walks through the shelter, she spots people in different areas who appear ''out of it''
and some that appear ''weird''.

This make mia think back to some of times she was
with linda when linda was doing drugs in a simi-
lar place and tears roll down her face.

INT. HOMELESS SHELTER - MOMENTS LATER

Mia lays curled up in a bed .... crying .... her
head and body completely under the cheap blue
blanket she was given when she got there.

EXT. HIGH SCHOOL - DAY

Mia waits at the front of the school clearly
looking for someone as the bell rings. kids pour
of the school but obviously not who Mia wants to
see as she exasperatedly storms off.

EXT. NEIGHBORHOOD STREET - LATER

Mia wears an expression of urgency as she talks
into her cellphone and walks up the street.

                    MIA
     Please call me. we need to talk.
     please.

EXT. APARTMENT COMPLEX COURTYARD - NIGHT

Mia slowly drags herself through the red brick
courtyard. she is extremely UNSTEADY as she looks
down at her cellphone.

with a gut-wrenching SOB Mia drops her phone in a
bush and rushes toward her apartment.

INT. APARTMENT - MOMENTS LATER

Mia enters the apartment and looks to see if anyone is there.

she's all alone.

INT. MIA'S ROOM -CONTINOUS

Mia goes into her room, grabs a scratch pad and
scribbles a note on it. she glances at her SHELF
OF TROPHIES but CRIES and quickly rushes out of
the room.

INT. BEDROOM 2 - MOMENTS LATER

Breathing heavily, Mia enters the room, heads
toward the closets but stops in her tracks as she

stares at a PHOTO of john and linda smiling happily ..... hanging on the wall.

Mia grabs the photo off the wall... looks at it for a moment. Then suddenly, she angrily smashes it on the floor and goes into the closets.

INT. CLOSET - CONTINOUS

Mia frantically searches the closet.... opening and tossing shoe boxes off the top shelf until..... she reaches into one shoe box and stops... pulling out a **GLOCK 9MM.**

As Mia studies the gun, her expression fluctuates between fear and peace.

Mia begins to breathe hard again. disengages the SAFETY, and then turns off the light. in complete darkness, Mia mumbles to herself and her breathing becomes frenetic.... almost like she's hyperventilating and sobbing at the same time.

Suddenly.... BANG!!!

END FLASHBACK

INT. HOSPITAL - ICU - EVENING

Mia's body jerks .... almost like she was reliving the gunshot to the head all over again.

The monitors start to beep and linda rushes to Mia's side.

                    LINDA
        Hold on, Me- Me. please.... don't go.

As suddenly as they began .... the monitors stop beeping.

                    LINDA (CONT'D)
Oh, thank God.

shannon stands at the door watching all that's going on.

                    JOHN
You know, Linda... if you showed her his this much love in years' past.... maybe she wouldn't have tried to blow her brains out.

Linda loses it!

                    LINDA
You asshole!!! i won't let you hurt us anymore.

                    JOHN
It's okay... i'm done away.

                    JOHN
It's okay...i'm done anyway.

Linda sheds a wildly devious grin.

                    LINDA
Truer words never been spoken.

Linda goes into her purse and pulls out the GLOCK 9MM Mia used to shoot herself and points it at john.

                    SHANNON
Linda, no! He's not worth going to jail for.

BANG! Linda shoots john in the chest and he immediately drops to the ground.

                    LINDA
    (looking at Mia)
    But she is.

Suddenly, Mia's monitor alarm.... something is
wrong this time as Doctor Green and a team of
Nurse rush into the room but stop short as they
see linda holding the gun and john

Laying on the floor in a pool of blood.

                HEAD NURSE
    Mrs. Daniels', your daughter needs

    attention but that means you need to

    put down the gun.

                    LINDA
    Shuts up, Tramp! Did you think i wouldn't
    smell him on you too?

One of the other Nurses bravely goes to check
Mia's condition

                    NURSE
    She's coding. Multiple organ failure. Her
    heart can't take it.

                DOCTOR GREEN
    Mia's going to need a kidney transplant.
    Mrs Daniels', you are the best candidate
    for the transplant. Please.... put down
    the gun.

                    LINDA
  I can't i'm sorry.

                DOCTOR GREEN
  Mia will die, Mrs. Daniels.

Linda puts the gun down and starts sobbing.

                    LINDA
  I'm not Mia's biological mother.

  She's adopted.

Shannon stares at the incredulous scene as police
officers enter and restrain Linda.

The medical team rushes into the action, trying
to save Mia's life. As they work on her, one of
the nurses uncovers Mia's upper body so they can
use the defibrillator on her heart.

As shannon looks on ..... her eye get HUGE as she
spots a HEART - SHAPED BIRTHMARK on Mia's chest!

                   SHANNON
  oh my God! It's her!

                DOCTOR GREEN
  We're losing her!

In Mia's mind she quickly begins to recall many
of the comments people have made to her about how
they see her.

                 BROOKE (V. O)
  I was weak and afraid. And you....i wish i
  was as strong as you were....

                    PK (V. O)
You are something else, Mia.

                  TRACY(V. O)
Please forgive me, cousin.

                  LINDA (V. O)
You .... are an amazing daughter. so smart...
creative.... and strong.

(smirks)

Much stronger than me.

Mia's monitors flat line. one by one, the medical
team stops working on her.

                  DOCTOR GREEN
    she's gone.

    (beat)

    call it.

                  HEAD NURSE
Time of death.... 11:11 pm.

Shannon looks on.... tears streaming down her
face. As the medical team exists the room, shannon crosses to Mia and whispers in her ear.

                  SHANNON (CONT'D)
    I love you.

FADE TO BLACK.

AS THE CREDITS ROLL.... A HEARTBEAT BEGINGS .....

The cast will give their thoughts on suicide,
predatory actions, drug abuse.

SUCIDE - With suicide, most times you don't get a second chance. so.... it is important to make the right choice when you have the chance. Never give in. Never lose hope. Things are NEVER as bad as they seem. talk to someone. You are strong enough... with God!

THE END???